Love Blooms
at the
Apple Blossom Inn

Tracy Fredrychowski

ISBN 978-1-7342411-5-0 (paperback)
ISBN 978-1-7342411-4-3 (digital)

Cover Design by Tracy Lynn, LLC

Cover background Photograph by Jim Fisher

All Bible verses taken from the New Life Version Bible (NLV) and the New King James Version (NKJV)

Published in South Carolina by The Tracer Group, LLC

https://tracyfredrychowski.com

To my mom, Priscilla:

Thank you for instilling in me a love for baking.

Our family cookbook will always be one of my most treasured items.

To my dad, James:

Thank you for teaching me to appreciate the simpler side of life.

Gardening, farming, and country pleasures are embedded in my soul.

Contents

A Note about Amish Vocabulary

The language the Amish speak is called Pennsylvania Dutch and is usually spoken rather than written. The spelling of commonly used words varies from community to community throughout the United States and Canada. Even as I researched for this book, the spelling of some words changed within the same Amish community that inspired this story. In one case, spellings were debated between family members. The words may have slightly different spellings, but all come from the interactions I've had with the people in the Amish settlement near where I was raised in Northwestern Pennsylvania.

While this book was modeled upon a small Amish community in Lawrence County, this is a work of fiction. The names and characters are products of my imagination and do not resemble any person, living or dead, or actual events that took place in that community.

List of Characters

Maggie Fisher. The oldest sibling in the Fisher household. Twenty-four-year-old Maggie is forced to travel across the country in hopes of finding a suitable husband.

Henry Schrock. Out of duty to his family, Henry works in his family's construction business. When a job in Willow Springs needs his attention, he takes it as a chance to convince Bella to return to Elkhart and her Amish heritage.

Mrs. Sorensen. Owner of the Apple Blossom Inn and a curt and demanding business owner.

Mr. George Waldorf. Business tycoon from New York interested in helping Mrs. Sorensen drive traffic to the Inn.

Mrs. Norma Waldorf. Soft-spoken wife to George.

Lizzie and Teena Fisher. The spinster great-aunts to Maggie. Best known as the community matchmakers.

Bella Fleming. Twenty-two-year-old Amish girl from Elkhart, Indiana, looking to find her way in the English world.

Amanda Beiler. Amish employee at the Apple Blossom Inn.

Chapter 1

Sugar Cookies

Maggie Fisher stood on the porch, potholders in hand looking through the glass of the wood-fired double oven. The sheltered porch did little to stop the Central Wisconsin wind from sending clouds of powdered snow up under her skirt. The outdoor kitchen her *datt* built five years ago was a welcomed relief to the summer heat but did little to warm her in the coldest months of the year.

A soft glow was starting to peek its way above the horizon, and it wouldn't be long before the first of their regular Friday customers began to make their way up the long winding driveway that led to their in-home bakery. Her oldest *bruder* was already clearing the snow from the driveway, and Hannah, her youngest *schwester,* was busy putting whipped frosting between layers of chocolate hand pies. Maggie smiled as she thought how it took the whole family to make sure the bakery opened by eight every morning, except Sundays, of course.

Cracking the oven door just far enough to see if the edges of the sugar cookies were the perfect golden brown, she reached in and lightly touched her finger in the center of the cookie checking if they were done. Glancing up at the timer she rarely used. A longing filled her heart as she remembered how her *mamm* had joked about neither of them needing a timer; they both instinctively knew something was done by how it smelled. She couldn't explain it, and neither could her *mamm,* that was before she died two years earlier. After placing the hot cookie trays on the baker's rack near the door, it would only take a few minutes before they were cooled and ready to frost.

Hearing the squeak of the rusty hinges, she turned her head in the direction of Hannah's voice.

"*Datt* is headed out to the barn and said he wants to talk to you when you're caught up. I can take those if you want." Hannah said as she reached for one of the trays.

"The barn, why would he want me to go there? He knows I need to finish these cookies. The shop opens in less than an hour. Oh, help!"

Pulling her heavy black coat tighter around her middle, she walked down the steps and tucked her chin close to her chest, bracing herself against the wind that whipped across the open yard.

The pungent odor of manure mixed with the sweet smell of hay tickled her nose as soon as she pushed the heavy steel door open. Steam rose from the nostrils of the full uttered Brown Swiss cows that lined either side of the barn. Milking all forty cows twice a day by hand, her *datt* and *bruders* worked filling ten-gallon milk cans that lined the milk house wall. Every ounce, except the little he let her keep, to make cheese and butter for the bakery, was sold to the cheese factory in town.

Walking to where her *datt* sat with his head rested on the side of a cow, she waited until he stood to empty his bucket before she spoke.

"Hannah said you wanted to see me."

Carrying the silver bucket with him, he motioned his head in the direction of the milk house and didn't say a word but expected her to follow. Once inside the clean small cinder block addition, he poured the bucket of fresh milk through the filtered lined bucket in the stainless steel sink.

"Shut the door," he said in a gruff voice.

Waiting patiently for him to get to his point, she tried not to seem aggravated that he had interrupted her baking. He was a man of few words, and she knew all too well not to rush him.

Turning to face her, he crossed his arms over his chest and leaned back on the sink and asked, "You'll be twenty-four next month, right?"

"I suppose so, why?"

Picking up the towel that hung over the edge of the sink, he said,

"It's time you find a husband."

Shocked by his comment, it took her a few seconds to fully comprehend what he said before she answered. "What for?"

"What do you mean, what for? I'm sure your *mamm* had that talk with you a long time ago."

Not typically prone to embarrassment, she couldn't help but blush at her *datt's* mention of the '*talk*.'

"I know that," she said in a hushed tone. "I mean, why do you think I need a husband now? There's too much to do around here to worry about such things."

Standing up straight and turning to check on the milk that was trickling through the layers of cheesecloth, he said, "My point exactly. As long as you're busy taking care of this family, you won't make time to start one of your own."

"But I don't mind. I love baking, and I wouldn't dream of letting *Mamm's* bakery business go."

With a stern voice, he answered, "Hannah is more than capable of taking over the bakery, so I'm sending you to your Aunts in Pennsylvania.

"To Willow Springs?" she said in a louder than respectable tone.

"You leave on the Greyhound first thing Monday morning. A driver will take you to the bus station, and your Great Aunts will secure a driver to pick you up in New Castle. You should arrive late Tuesday afternoon."

Trying to control the heaviness creeping up in her chest, she decided to soften her tone before she continued. "But *Datt,* what on earth am I going to do in Willow Springs? I don't know anyone there, and all I know about Aunt Teena and Lizzie is they're spinsters. If they couldn't find a husband there, what makes you think I will?"

"Not sure you will. Especially since you've chased every boy within twenty miles of this place away with your sharp tongue. I'm figuring if I send you to a new town, your reputation might not follow you, and there might be some fellow willing to give you a try."

"*Datt,* how can you say such things?"

"Can you prove me wrong?"

Not answering his question, but pleading with him, she said, "But you need me around here."

"As I said, Hannah is plenty old enough, and I'll be chasing her off this farm as well someday."

Lowering herself to a milking stool near the door, she propped her elbows on her knees and rested her chin in her palms. Looking up at him, she said, "You can't be serious."

"Look, I promised your *mamm* I wouldn't expect you to fill her shoes forever. It's been two years now; it's time."

Shifting his weight and running his hand through his brown and white speckled beard, he said, "You have a job waiting for you at the Apple Blossom Inn."

Pouring the filtered milk in the waiting can, he secured the lid, picked up the empty bucket, and headed toward the door. Stopping only long enough to say, "You have many wonderful qualities, but your eagerness to always have the last word ...well, that might take a special kind of man."

Letting his words sink in, he paused in the doorway to add, "For sure and certain, you won't find him here in Tomah."

As if she was frozen to the stool, Maggie didn't move even after her *datt* had long gone. Thinking to herself, she thought. *How can he send me off to live in a strange town, with people I barely know, it's plain crazy! The last thing I need right now is a husband.*

The way she saw it, he didn't hold much hope of her finding a suitable mate in her community. All her friends were already married with children of their own, but she was hardly spinster material. Or was she?

~~

Monday morning came quickly, and the goodbyes were harder than she imagined. However, she knew her siblings were more than capable of keeping the bakery running and helping *Datt* on the farm.

Only five hours into her twenty-hour bus ride, and she was already missing home. Outside the bus window, the flat windmill littered landscape of northern Indiana didn't do anything to soothe her wounded spirit. The bleak gray of winter matched her mood identically. The thought of her *datt* being so quick to send her away without considering her feelings left her dismayed.

Closing her eyes and laying her head against the cold window, she tried to create a picture of her sweet *mamm.* Every time she thought of her, she had to push the memories of her sick in bed aside and remember the good times they had. Time spent baking and gardening together. They shared a love for baking, but their personalities were the complete opposite. Hers was more like her *datt's,* with his quick wit and bossy exterior. The only difference being, it was alright for a man, but not for a woman. Something she failed to learn on her own yet.

It wasn't that she wouldn't enjoy accepting a buggy ride home from a Sunday evening youth gathering, but she hadn't met any boy that enjoyed her playful bantering. The way she saw it, most of the boys in her Old-Order Community wanted a wife that would be seen and not heard. God willing, she'd be able to find a man who allowed her a voice of her own. Reasoning with herself, being the oldest girl of twelve children, she needed to be a bit bossy and sometimes even a know-it-all to keep order in a family that size.

Opening her eyes when the bus driver announced they'd be stopping in Elkhart, Indiana, she focused her attention out the window as semi after semi passed them on Interstate 90. She had never been this far from home and surrounded by so many strangers at that. She may be almost twenty-four, but she had never ventured more than twenty-five miles from home. A little part of her was excited about the adventure, but a big part of her wanted nothing more than to be back home, baking bread, and taking care of her family.

Pulling into the hotel parking lot that doubled as a curbside bus station, she waited her turn to exit the bus and stretch her legs. Pulling her heavy black bonnet snug around her chin, she walked up and down the sidewalk, rubbing her hands together for warmth. Keeping a close eye on the bus, she took the time to take in the surroundings. Maybe traveling to Pennsylvania wasn't so bad after all, it was forcing her out of her comfort zone. Pulling her black purse draped over her shoulder tighter, she remembered the money her *datt* had given her, along with specific instructions to keep it close.

The dark clouds above wasted no time in letting a new dusting of snow cover her black bonnet, forcing her to find warmth back on the bus. Settling back into her seat near the window, she continued to watch passengers check their tickets with the driver and find a place. The last one to enter was a young man who appeared close to her age. His wide-brimmed black hat and wool coat gave her comfort in a way she couldn't explain. Dropping her head just as he turned to look toward the back of the bus, she waited until he took a seat before lifting her head. He settled into a seat near the window and removed his jacket and hat and lay them in the seat beside him. She took notice of the way his dark hair had matted a circle around his head, and the ends had flipped up in small waves even after he removed his hat. She caught a glimpse of his purple collar and wondered what community allowed such a vivid shade of violet. Wishing her community allowed such worldly colors; purple was one of her favorites.

For the next four hours, she stared at the back of his head, wondering all kinds of things that she hadn't allowed herself to daydream about in a very long time. Only when the bus driver came on the intercom to say they would be stopping in Toledo, Ohio did she shake her head and push the thoughts of the dark-haired stranger from her mind.

Pulling her ticket from her purse and reading through the stops listed on it, she noticed her layover would be eight hours. Taking in a deep breath, she wondered what on earth she'd do for such a long time. Nibbling on her bottom lip, she remembered the promise she made to her *datt* to stay close to the bus and not talk to strangers.

After the bus came to a complete stop, the driver instructed them to check their tickets for the time of their connecting bus. He mentioned this was his last stop, and they all would need to exit the bus. Again, her stomach churned with thoughts of sitting for eight hours with nothing to do. She packed a few sandwiches but wasn't in the least bit hungry. Once the driver opened the door, she gathered her belongings and stood to put her jacket on. As she tied her bonnet around her chin, she glanced at the gentleman who captured her attention. He stood and turned in her direction. Placing his hat back on his head, he tipped the rim and nodded at her as he caught her looking his way. In an instant, her face warmed as she glanced away before he realized she'd been watching him.

Letting all the passengers file out first, she was the last to pick up her suitcase waiting on the curb. Following everyone through the double doors and into the station, she stood off to the side, taking in the cold room. Looking for a seat, she headed to the corner, away from the most congested areas. Glancing at the location of the arrival and departure screen, it didn't take long for her to understand the computerized chart. Looking toward the washroom and then down at her bags, she was surprised when a voice behind her said, "You can leave your bags with me if you'd like."

Turning toward the voice, she found herself staring back into the stormy gray eyes of the stranger on the bus. Unable to speak, she grunted something inaudible and carried her bags in the direction of the women's restroom. Once inside and away from his eyes, she leaned up against the wall and caught her breath. Lightly bouncing the back of her head off the wall, she thought to herself. *What was that all about? Since when do I open my mouth, and nothing comes out? Maybe I can just stay here until it's time for my bus to leave.*

Looking around the dimly lit room, staying in the dirty restroom wasn't an option. Locating an open seat, she scanned the room for the familiar dark hair. When her search didn't reveal his location, she pushed the small brown leather suitcase under her chair, giving ample room for someone to sit beside her if need be. Reaching for the book from her bag, she found her marked spot and blocked out everything around her and escaped to the story inside.

It had only been a few minutes into her book before she caught a glimpse of the man as he sat beside her. Trying to act as if she didn't notice him, she pulled her legs in tight, refusing to acknowledge his presence. Trying to keep her attention in the book, she became frustrated at reading the same sentence twice, forcing her to close it and lay it on her lap.

As he draped his heavy jacket over his knee, the movement released the distinctive aroma of burned wood. It reminded her of her *datt* after he'd been outside stoking the furnace on a rainy day. Her stomach flipped as she thought he smelled just like a man should.

Turning in her seat away from him, she closed her eyes and tried to push the crazy thoughts from her head. Why on earth was she thinking all these things about a stranger she hadn't even met? Embarrassed by her reaction to him, she picked up her belongings and moved to a seat across the room.

Minutes dragged on forever as the clock ticked away one hour at a time. All she wanted was to continue her journey. Far away from the man that captivated her thoughts in an unladylike manner. Allowing herself to look his way one last time, she followed his broad shoulders out the door to the bus headed to Akron.

Chapter 2

Honey Wheat White Bread

With a gentle nudge from the woman next to her, Maggie opened her eyes when the older woman said, "I believe this is your stop. New Castle, right?"

"Yes, it is." She answered as she looked out the window. "Oh my, I must have slept for three hours. I'm sorry I wasn't much company for you." Maggie said as she gathered her purse and canvas bag.

"No problem, I nodded off as well." Standing to let her by, she continued in a whisper, "I hope you find what you're looking for in Pennsylvania."

"I will put that in God's hands and His alone. It was nice to meet you and thank you for listening to me. I'm sorry if I talked too much." Maggie said as she hurried by.

"You have no idea how much I enjoyed it. It was nice to have someone to talk to for the last twelve hours and thank you for sharing your sandwiches with me. As I said, you should sell that recipe; it was the best I've ever tasted, and I should be thanking you." The petite silver haired woman said.

Startled when the woman pulled her into a hug and whispered in her ear. "Blessings await all those who trust in the Lord."

The woman's soft touch and calming voice gave her a comfort she hadn't felt in a very long time. "Thank you again; it was a pleasure getting to know you. Stay safe on the rest of your journey, and I hope you enjoy your visit with your grandchildren."

Stepping off the bus and into the bright sunshine, Maggie shifted her purse and tote bag to pick up the suitcase the bus driver left on the curb. Looking around for any signs of her ride, she walked to the covered waiting area to escape the cold. Before she had a chance to drop her bags, a middle-aged woman approached her. "Margaret Fisher?"

"Yes, are you my ride?"

"I'm Shelby; your Aunts sent me for you. They're so excited you've come to stay with them."

Putting her suitcase in the trunk of the woman's waiting car, she opened the back door just as Shelby said, "Don't be silly; sit in the front seat with me."

Walking to the front of the car, Maggie wasted no time getting in and away from the wind.

"Burr," Maggie said as she rubbed her hands together. "I'll sure be glad when warmer weather gets here. I've had just about enough of the cold. It's as bad here as in Wisconsin."

"Me too, I hope spring gets here soon."

Shelby kept the conversation going. "So, what brings you to Willow Springs?"

Taking a few seconds to answer, Maggie said, "My *datt* said it was time I come and meet my Great Aunts. I've never met them personally."

"Well, you're in for a treat, they're two of my favorite people." Letting out a slight giggle before she continued, she said, "Their shenanigans in matchmaking are known around these parts. I'd say they're responsible for about fifty percent of the marriages in Willow

Springs. Last year they locked Barbara and Joseph in a stockroom and low and behold they're getting married next month."

Maggie laced her fingers together on her lap and squeezed her hands tight as she thought. *That's why he sent me here.*

Without saying a word, she looked straight ahead and listened as Shelby pointed things out as they passed. "We're only about twenty minutes from your Aunts house. They tell me you have a job waiting at the Apple Blossom Inn. We'll pass that on our way."

Not wanting to seem rude, she smiled and nodded, trying to seem interested in Shelby's chatter. Hearing that her aunts were known for matchmaking left a nervous pit in the bottom of her stomach. She couldn't help but think her *datt* set this up knowing what they were known for.

Slowing down and pointing to a white Victorian house, Shelby said, "There's the Apple Blossom Inn. We're only about a half of a mile from Lizzie and Teena's."

"How pretty," Maggie said as she followed Shelby's gaze out the window. "I'm not sure what I'll be doing yet, but I'm thankful my Aunts found me a job."

Shelby sped back up as she said, "The woman who owns the Inn is a little brassy around the edges, but don't let her scare you. She has a heart as big as a warm apple pie when it comes down to it."

"Well, here we are," Shelby said as she pulled in the driveway of the little white house that sat hidden behind three full pine trees.

Maggie smiled as she unlatched her seat belt and pushed open her door. The quaint little cottage had a warm feel about it. The smoke that swirled from the chimney and its robin's egg blue colored door welcomed her before she set foot on the porch. Taking her suitcase from Shelby's hand, she asked, "What do I owe you?"

"Already taken care of, so we're good." Waving to the two women who stood in the doorway, she whispered, "Enjoy your time in Willow Springs and watch out for those two. They'll have you married off with babies quicker than you can shake a stick."

Walking toward the house and into her new life, Maggie gave a nervous smile to the two older women who were eagerly awaiting her arrival.

~~

After placing her things in the room they directed her to, she found her way back to the kitchen.

"I think I'm all settled. Thank you again for allowing me to stay here. I hope I'm not too much trouble."

"Too much trouble? Absolutely not." Lizzie said. "We're glad to have you. It's been way too long since we've had anyone visit."

The other woman stood and poured hot water in the cup in front of her and asked, "Do you take honey or sugar in your tea?"

"Honey," she said as she opened a tea bag and let it steep in the hot liquid.

Bouncing the tea bag up and down in her cup, Maggie said, "I'm a little embarrassed to ask, but I'm not sure which one of you is Aunt Teena and which is Lizzie."

"Oh, help! Lizzie said. "Silly me. I'm Lizzie, and that makes her Teena."

Teena was quick to add, "Your *datt's* oldest aunt to be exact, which makes me his youngest."

Lizzie replied in a sassy tone. "Now, don't go splitting hairs; I might be the oldest but still the wisest by far."

Maggie stirred a spoon of honey in her cup and asked, "So tell me about the Apple Blossom Inn. *Datt* says you've lined up a job for me."

Lizzie broke off a piece of cookie that sat on a plate between them and said, "There was a notice in the window at Shetler's Grocery a couple of weeks ago, so we stopped by and spoke with Mrs. Sorensen at the Inn."

Teena finished her *schwester's* sentence as soon as Lizzie put the cookie in her mouth. "We told her you were coming, and you'd need a job. She's holding the position until she interviews you. She is expecting you first thing in the morning."

"Do you know what I'll be doing?"

Tilting her head and rubbing her chin, Teena answered, "I'm not sure." Looking in Lizzie's direction, she asked, "Do you remember if she said what the job was?"

Lizzie thought for a moment before she answered. "I don't think she said. I would assume it's cooking or cleaning. Many girls in the community worked for her at one time or another and that's what they've done."

Teena dipped a cookie into her cup as she said, "It doesn't seem like she keeps anyone too long. Never did understand why she goes through help like she does."

Lizzie patted the back of Maggie's hand and said, "I'm sure you'll do fine at whatever job she gives you."

Without barely taking a breath, Lizzie changed the subject. "So, tell us about your family. What is our nephew Josiah up to these days? His letters are always short and sweet, but we never really know how he's doing after your *mamm* passed."

In a quiet tone, Maggie answered, "We all miss her. What gets to me the most is the babies hardly remember her. They were nearly two when she died."

Teena shook her head side to side and said, "All in God's plan for sure and certain."

"*Datt* doesn't say much, but we can tell he misses her. We find him sitting alone on the porch most evenings."

Stopping to take a drink of her tea, she held her cup with both hands to her lips and said, "He wears his pain on his face as plain as day."

The thought of watching her *datt* as he struggled to live his life without her still brought tears to her eyes. Wiping the moisture from her eye with the back of her hand, she continued, "I guess we've all found ways to keep her memories alive. I've been able to keep her bakery business going, and my younger *schwester's* have taken to tending to the babies."

"Oh Margaret, it's such a shame they won't even remember her," Teena said in a caring voice.

Letting a small gasp from in the back of her throat Maggie said, "No one has called me Margaret since *Mamm* died. She was the only one to call me by my given name. To everyone else, I'm Maggie."

"Did you know your great grandmother's name was Margaret?" Teena asked.

"Really? No, I guess I didn't. What was she like?"

Lizzie pushed herself away from the table and said, "She was as sharp as a nail, tough as an old rooster, and had a quick tongue. You didn't want to cross her."

Teena laughed and said, "Now *schwester,* she wasn't all that bad. Look how she mellowed out as she got older. She lived with us for years after *Datt* passed, and she was a pleasant addition to our little home."

Lizzie was quick to add in a snippy tone. "Being the youngest, you don't remember her as I do. I was the oldest, and she was harder on me than she was with you. By the time you came along, she was tired and let you do as you please. Even *Datt* said as much."

“Even so, I was pleased when you were named Margaret. I remember how happy it made her when she found out she had a namesake." Teena said in a pleasing voice.

Maggie rubbed the rim of her cup and guestioned, "Just the other day, *Datt* told me I had a sharp tongue as well. Maybe that's where I got it from."

"Could be," Lizzie answered as she carried her cup to the sink.

Maggie stood up and pushed her chair under the table and said, "If you both don't mind, I think I'm going to go lay down for a bit. I barely slept last night, and the few hours I did on the bus weren’t enough."

"By all means, go make yourself comfortable. You should find everything you need in your room, and if not, you let us know." Teena said as she shooed her away with the back of her hand.

~~

Maggie slept through dinner and didn't wake until peaks of sunlight started to filter into her room. Opening her eyes and trying to make sense of her strange surroundings, it took a few seconds before she remembered where she was. Pulling the windup clock closer, she jumped out of bed when it read eight. Her interview was at nine, and she didn't want to be late. Wasting no time in dressing, she made her way back to the kitchen in time for Aunt Lizzie to hand her a cup of tea.

"I was just heading in to wake you. We let you sleep last night, but we didn't want you to be late for your meeting with Mrs. Sorensen."

Pulling her boots on over her stockings and putting her shoes in the tote, she said, "I can't believe I slept so long. I guess the long trip from Tomah got to me more than I thought. How far is it to the Inn?"

Teena pushed a bowl of oatmeal in front of her and said, "It will only take you about fifteen minutes to walk there, so you have plenty of time for a proper breakfast."

"Are you sure? I'd hate to be late."

"I'm certain," Teena said. "Now, take a few minutes and turn around and eat."

Closing her eyes and saying a silent prayer over her oatmeal before she continued, she asked, "How cold is it outside?"

Lizzie pulled the pleated blue curtain away from the window at the sink and said, "Twenty-seven degrees. Perfect walking weather. Take that blue scarf from the hook and wrap it around your neck, and you'll be good." Turning from the window and walking to her chair at the table, she added, "Fresh air always does a body good, is what our *datt* always said. Right, Teena?"

"For sure and certain," Teena replied.

~~

Aunt Lizzie was right; fresh air was what she needed. After her long sleep and the brisk walk, Maggie felt ready to start her new routine in Willow Springs.

Stopping in front of the Inn, she marveled at the beauty of the stunning white structure. The wrap around porch and fancy woodwork gave the Inn a majestic feel. She couldn't think of any old houses in Tomah that looked as pretty. The stark white wooden siding stood out against the bluebird sky. She smiled as she made her way up the driveway and onto the front porch. She was excited to work in such a fancy house.

Stopping on the front porch to take note of the white wicker chairs and potted planters filled with pine boughs, she marveled that everything looked perfect.

Slowly opening the door and walking into the foyer, she was in awe of the beautifully carved staircase that led to the second floor. A calming smell of a spice she couldn't place, along with burning wood and freshly brewed coffee, filled her nose. The Inn was nothing like any home she'd ever been to, and its warmth invited her in and surrounded her the minute she opened the door.

Not sure where she should go, she took a moment to take off her coat and drape it over her arm. Wiping her snow-covered boots off on the rug at the door, she slipped them off and put on her shoes. Heels clicking on the polished wood floor alerted her to the dark-haired woman standing in front of her.

"Margaret Fisher, I assume?"

"Yes, but I prefer Maggie."

"Is Margaret your name?"

"Yes, ma'am."

"Then it's Margaret in my book. I'll never understand why people don't go by their given names."

Turning to walk down the long hallway that led to the back of the house, the older woman didn't look back but said, "Are you coming? I don't have all day."

Keeping up with her quick strides, Maggie followed her as she walked through the house with a sense of style and grace. Her posture was perfect, and even the swoosh of her silk pants echoed off the walls, giving everything in her path a sense of control.

Pointing to the brown leather chair in front of the desk, she instructed Maggie to take a seat with a flick of her finger.

Laying her coat across the back of the chair, Maggie got comfortable while she waited for the woman to speak.

Without the usual pleasantries, Mrs. Sorensen got right to the point.

"How old are you?"

"I'll be twenty-four next month."

Raising an eyebrow and looking over the rim of her glasses, she guestioned, "Married?"

"No, ma'am."

"Plan on it?"

"Excuse me?"

In an aggravated tone, Mrs. Sorensen asked, "Do you plan on getting married?"

Trying to understand why she would want to know such a personal matter; Maggie took a few seconds before she answered. "Not anytime soon. But maybe someday."

"Good. It seems like every girl I hire leaves me for some fellow shortly after she starts working. You wouldn't believe how many Amish girls leave me in a lurch."

Crossing her legs and replying in a confident tone, Maggie said, "I can assure you I don't have any fellow looking to steal me away anytime soon."

Without lifting her head from the clipboard she was writing on, she continued.

"I need someone to be my girl Friday."

"Girl Friday? Not sure what that means." Maggie asked.

"It means I need someone to do a variety of jobs and be my backup when I'm not here. I need someone I can give a job list to in the morning and expect it done before she leaves. I need someone to run errands and do whatever I ask." Pausing to sit back in her chair and wait for a response, she added, "Is that you?"

Learning quick, Mrs. Sorensen liked strong character; Maggie replied in a poised tone, "It could be if you'll give me a chance."

Sitting up straighter, Maggie looked Mrs. Sorensen straight in the eye and said, "I'm confident I won't disappoint you. I'm great at multitasking and pick things up quickly."

Leaning forward in her chair, Mrs. Sorensen tapped a pencil on the clipboard in front of her and said, "Well, I'll be the judge of that."

Not even pausing to let Maggie answer, she tucked the pencil behind her ear. The tight bun that held her salt and pepper hair back didn't so much as budge. "There are two things I expect of all of my employees. One, you are to be seen and not heard. I expect our guests to feel well cared for. Be available but not noticed. Number two, you are to use the service entrance at the back of the house. The front door is for guests only." Looking up to make sure she was listening, she added, "Do you understand?"

"I do."

"Good, then you can start by working on this list. You can ask me any questions, but I'm counting on you being smart enough to figure things out on your own. I don't want to babysit you. Is that clear?"

"Yes, Ma'am."

Waiting to be dismissed, Maggie was startled when she continued sharply, "Well? What are you waiting for? Get to it." She added as she pointed to the door.

Picking up her coat and grabbing the clipboard, she took her things to the back hall. Taking only a second to sit on the bench at the back door, she glanced over the items on her list before making her way to the kitchen. As she walked past Mrs. Sorensen's open-door, she called her name. "Margaret."

Stopping and backing up, she peered around the corner of the door and said, "Yes?"

"Two of my loyal guests, Mr. and Mrs. Waldorf, are visiting with us for the next few weeks, and I want them handled with kid gloves. They send a lot of business my way, and I want them taken care of.

Before you start your list, please go to the parlor and see to it they have everything they need."

"You can count on it," was all she said before she headed back down the hall. Only taking a few steps, Mrs. Sorensen hollered, "Make sure you put on one of the pink aprons hanging in the supply closet in the kitchen first."

Chapter 3

Vanilla Scones

Tying the pink apron securely around her waist, Maggie headed in the direction of the parlor. Taking in a deep breath, trying to prepare herself for her first task, she headed to the front of the Inn. Stopping in the doorway between the parlor and the dining room, she glanced at the older couple sitting in leather chairs near the window in the mauve-colored room. A warm fire burned in the fireplace, and soft music played in the background. Mr. Waldorf was flipping through pages of the newspaper, and Mrs. Waldorf was working a needle through thin fabric pulled tightly on a small round frame.

Clearing her throat to announce her arrival, she said, "Mrs. Sorensen ask me to check on you both. May I bring you something warm to drink, or do you need anything?"

The petite, gray-haired woman lifted her head, smiled, and then answered, "That would be lovely. A cup of tea would be nice, and maybe one of those scones I saw on the buffet in the dining room." Turning to address her husband, she said, "George, do you want this young lady to bring you anything?"

Without answering her question, he said, "Can you believe Global Bakery stock is up fifteen points today? I told Marshall he should have bought that stock last year when it was low." Snapping his paper and holding it up, hiding his face, he went back to reading, mumbling something under his breath as he ignored his wife's' question.

Laying her needlepoint on her lap, she looked up at Maggie and said, "Don't mind George; he gets all worked up over the Stock Market. We're supposed to be on holiday, but it's hard for him to leave work behind. He's even gone as far as to set up an appointment with someone while we're here."

Curious, Maggie asked, "What kind of work do you do? If you don't mind me asking."

"George, the girl is asking you a question."

Peering out around the side of his paper, he said sharply. "Do you know anything about the bakery business?"

"My family runs an in-home bakery in Wisconsin. Do you own a bakery?"

Without giving him ample time to answer, she cut her conversation short as Mrs. Sorensen called for her from the hallway.

"I believe I told you to tend to their needs, not pepper them with annoying questions." In a stern voice, she continued, "See to their needs and nothing else. Do you understand me this time?"

Alarmed that she had upset her so soon, Maggie dropped her head and said, "It won't happen again."

"Good, see to it that you don't become a bother. There's a shipment of flowers sitting on the counter in the kitchen. Gather up all the vases throughout the house and replace them with the fresh flowers that were just delivered. Be sure to snip the ends at an angle and make sure you use room temperature water."

Without hesitating, she headed to the dining room to gather a tray of tea and scones to take to their guests. Setting two cups and a plate of pastries on the tray, she couldn't help but wonder what kind of work Mr. Waldorf did, that had to do with a bakery. Not wanting to be on Mrs. Sorensen's wrong side, she'd keep her curiosity to herself.

Standing in front of Mrs. Waldorf, she waited as the older woman picked up a cup off the tray. "Thank you, dear, I love this tea. I hear she orders it from England. Is that true?"

"I just started work today, so I don't know, but I can ask."

Holding the cup up to her lips, Mrs.Waldorf blew the hot liquid and answered before taking a sip. "That won't be necessary. I love it no matter where she gets it."

Walking closer to where Mr. Waldorf sat, Maggie held the tray out so that he could retrieve a cup himself. Setting the cup on the stand between the chairs, he picked up a napkin and helped himself to one of the vanilla scones she offered him.

"I wonder if these are going to be as dry as they look." He said in a slightly sarcastic tone.

Mrs. Waldorf was quick to respond. "George, now don't be so picky, be happy you have a scone to eat and don't criticize it before you taste it. Not everyone is as experienced as you are, so be nice."

Watching as the gray-haired gentleman wrinkled up his nose as he took a bite, Maggie knew it would be dry before he even tasted it. Scones should be thick like her buttermilk biscuits not thin like a cookie. Thinking to herself, she wondered if she should say something to the baker or maybe to Mrs. Sorensen.

Shaking his head and putting the pastry back on the tray, he said, "Such a shame, it's hard to get a good scone unless I make them myself." Taking his hand and waving the tray away from him, he picked up his paper and hid behind the black and white print.

Without saying a word, Maggie carried the tray from the room and set it on the table in the dining room and broke off a piece to taste. He was right; it was dry, tasteless, and anything but appetizing. Not sure if she should mention it to Mrs. Sorensen, she carried the tray back to the kitchen in search of the flowers.

Locating the five-gallon bucket near the sink filled with flowers, she headed in its direction. The kitchen was empty, and she had yet to meet the person in charge of cooking. Remnants of the morning baking were still on the countertop as she ran her finger through the leftover flour. Laying off to the side was a recipe card with VANILLA SCONES printed across the top. Picking up the card and reading through the ingredients, she agreed with the measurements. Thinking to herself, she thought. *Could be the dough was worked too much, or the butter wasn't cold enough. I would have used cream instead of milk and a real vanilla bean instead of imitation. I think I may have used vanilla pudding to give them a distinctive flavor.*

Looking around to make sure no one saw her she opened the drawer in search of a pencil. Maybe if she added a few notes to the recipe card, the baker would have better results next time. Satisfied with the tips, she wrote on the card then returned it to its place on the counter and went in search of vases.

On her walk through the Inn, she marveled at the well cared for Victorian and took time to familiarize herself with its layout. Making her way through each room, gathering the vases that would soon hold fresh tulips and daffodils, she felt a sense of pride in working in such a beautiful place.

Mrs. Sorensen had a tough exterior that she would need to figure out, but the woman knew how to make the Inn feel homey and comfortable. As she made her way back to the kitchen, she stopped in the doorway as Mrs. Sorensen held the platter of scones. In a stern but hushed tone, she was reprimanding a young girl for the quality of her baked goods. Trying to stay out of their way, she made her way to the sink and the waiting bucket. Filling each vase with slightly warm water, she let them sit and went to work on snipping each end in the precise manner Mrs. Sorensen instructed her to.

Waiting until the older woman left the room, Maggie looked in the direction of the girl and watched as the ribbons from her *kapp* swayed as she emptied the tray of scones in the trash.

Holding a pair of floral shears in one hand and a long pink tulip in the other, she turned around and said, "We haven't gotten a chance to meet. My name is Maggie Fisher."

In a whisper, the girl said, "Amanda Beiler"

Amanda reached for a clean bowl and the recipe card that lay on the counter. Maggie waited as she read through the recipe and smiled as the girl pushed the dish of warm butter aside and retrieved cold butter and cream from the refrigerator.

Maggie stayed quiet as Amanda returned from the pantry with a jar of vanilla beans. She went back to her flowers and let the young girl try the recipe again.

Vanilla and sugar lingered in the air as Maggie strategically placed the fresh flowers throughout the Inn. Mr. and Mrs. Waldorf had returned to their room, and two new couples made their way into the dining room, waiting for breakfast. Satisfied she had completed the first assignment, she flinched at Mrs. Sorensen's sharp tone.

"Margaret."

Following the sound of her voice to the office, she stopped in the doorway.

"Three more guests are checking in this afternoon. One couple is here to attend an event at the college, and a young man has business with Mr. Waldorf. I need you to ready their rooms. Normally I have a housekeeper, but she up and quit on me yesterday. Until she's replaced, I'll need you to fill in. Do you have a problem with that?"

"No, Ma'am."

Watching the stern woman pull her glasses from the top of her head and perch them low on her nose, she said in an authoritative tone. "Good. Here is a cleaning checklist for each room."

Without lifting her head, she asked, "Any questions?"

"No, I believe I understand everything."

"Then what are you waiting for?" Pausing for only a second, she added, "On your way through the kitchen, remind Amanda I want to sample the new batch of scones before she serves them."

Maggie didn't respond but turned on her heels and headed in the direction of the kitchen.

~~

Stopping briefly to deliver the message, she inhaled the sweet aroma and glanced at the puffy warm scones cooling on the counter.

Picking up a napkin and reaching for one of the sweet buttery pastries, she asked, "May I?"

With a hopeful look on her face, Amanda nodded without saying a word.

Blowing on it before breaking off a small piece, she placed it in her mouth and savored its perfect texture before saying, "Oh my, Mrs. Sorensen will be happy with these. They're perfect."

Not waiting for the girls' response, she carried the sweet treat with her and headed up the stairs to begin her cleaning task. Trying to concentrate on the instructions detailed out on her clipboard, she couldn't help but feel a sense of pride in helping the girl. Wishing she was in the kitchen baking instead of upstairs cleaning, she unlocked the cleaning closet door and, with a heavy sigh, pulled the cleaning cart from the small room.

~~

Henry Schrock stepped off the bus and pulled his wide-brimmed wool hat down to block the early afternoon sun. Looking around for any sign of the driver hired to take him to the Apple Blossom Inn, he waited patiently for someone to approach him.

"Henry Schrock?"

"Yes, I'm Henry. Are you my driver?"

"I decided to come for you myself instead of hiring a driver." Mr. Waldorf extended his hand to introduce himself. "George Waldorf, at your service."

"I'm sorry I assumed you were my driver."

"My wife insisted I get out and stretch my legs. We are supposed to be on holiday, but I like to keep busy, and all this downtime is driving me crazy."

"Nice to meet you in person finally," Henry added sincerely.

Picking up his small brown leather suitcase, he followed Mr. Waldorf in the direction of his car parked across the street. Trying to keep up with the older gentleman's long strides, Henry wasted no time in following his lead.

Taking the keys from his pocket, Mr. Waldorf popped the trunk and instructed Henry to place his suitcase inside. Waiting for the lid to automatically shut, George added, "We've lots to discuss, but so far, Willow Springs will be the perfect place for me to build a franchise for Waldorf Bakery. I'm pleased you agreed to meet me here."

Henry slid into the front seat and took a moment to adjust to the plush interior and smooth leather before snapping his seat belt in place and continuing. "It was no trouble. I have family business to take care of, so it only made sense. Typically, my father would have come to meet you, but we have two big projects underway in Elkhart that he couldn't be pulled away from. I can assure you I can represent my father's business as well as he can."

Pulling his seat belt across his shoulder and snapping it in place, Mr. Waldorf stated, "We've wanted to venture into this area, and this town is perfect. It's close to the Interstate, and the Outlet Mall, which makes Willow Springs the perfect location. I originally wanted to find a location closer to the Interstate, but this sleepy little Amish Community might better suit me. I have the idea to staff it with Amish women and make it a tourist destination."

Pausing to back the car out of its parking spot and pull out on the highway, Mr. Waldorf settled into driving before he continued. "Schrock Construction comes highly recommended, but I'm concerned you don't have an office here in Northwestern Pennsylvania. How do you expect to handle the construction phase from Elkhart?"

Henry took his hat off and pushed his matted bangs off his forehead before answering. "That won't be a problem. If we can agree, I would act as General Contractor and stay on the job site until it's finished. We would hire a local Amish Construction company to complete the build and local tradespeople for the electrical and plumbing. I would serve as your point of contact and update you and answer any questions you would have during the construction."

Even though Mr. Waldorf seemed pleased with his answers, there was something about the way he wanted to exploit the Amish area that didn't sit well with Henry. He couldn't help but think it might hurt the businesses of the local bakeries if a franchise came to town. He made a mental note to check if there were any in-home bakeries in Willow Springs before he agreed to take on Mr. Waldorf's project.

Chapter 4

Apple Crisp

The ring of the front door alarm caught Maggie's attention as she pushed the cleaning cart back into the closet at the top of the stairs. The Inn had been quiet as she finished her task of preparing the rooms for the afternoon guests. Smoothing out her pink apron and tucking a few stray strands of wheat-colored hair under her *kapp*, she walked down the stairs just as Mr. Waldorf and his business guest made their way in the foyer.

Grabbing the polished wood railing, she caught her breath as she came face to face with the man who she memorized every curl on the back of his head. At that very moment, even if she wanted to say something, no sound escaped her lips.

Watching as the dark-haired man set his suitcase on the floor, he took off his hat and nodded in her direction. Even before she had a chance to say a word, Mrs. Sorensen called to them from the hallway.

"Welcome to the Apple Blossom Inn. You must be Henry Schrock; we've been expecting you."

"Margaret, take Mr. Schrock's bag to Room 6."

Without hesitating, she reached for his bag and kept her head down, trying to avoid acknowledging their brief familiarity with one another. Carrying the bag up the stairs, she sensed his eyes piercing her back, but was determined not to turn around. Only when she got to the top of the stairs did she stop and turn, secretly hoping to catch a glimpse of him from afar. She breathed a sigh of relief when she found the foyer empty.

Using her master key, she unlocked the door and placed his leather bag inside. Pausing in the doorway, she looked over the room to be sure everything was perfect. Going over the list in her head, she looked around the room, checking off each item.

The bed was made with tight corners. Fresh flowers were in the vase on the dresser. A small dish of wrapped chocolates sat on the stand near the chair by the fireplace. Clean towels and bath necessities were in the bathroom. Everything was perfect, just like Henry Schrock. Shaking her head, she tried to push all the crazy thoughts away as she mumbled to herself. *What's my problem, when did I become a mumbling idiot and all tongue-tied? Handsome or not, I'm not letting the likes of Henry Schrock get under my skin. And I'm certainly not going to give Datt the satisfaction of knowing I may have found an interesting prospect on day two. Absolutely NOT! I'll stay far away from him. Simple as that.*

Determined to stay clear of their new guest, she closed the door and tucked the key in her apron. Stopping halfway down the stairs, she listened carefully to the sound of the voices at the check-in desk at the end of the hall. Mrs. Sorensen and Mr. Waldorf's voices echoed against the walls, but Henry's wasn't in the mix. Not taking a chance in facing him, she quietly made her way down the stairs and headed through the parlor and down the long hallway that led to the back of the Inn.

Glancing over her shoulder, she walked straight into an open door. Hitting it so hard, she lost her balance, fell to the floor, and spread-eagle right in front of Henry. What seemed like minutes, but in all reality was only a couple seconds, she laid on the floor looking into the smokey gray eyes she was trying to avoid. Feeling her skirt hiked up above her knees, but frozen in his gaze, it was impossible for her to push the blue fabric down to a respectable length.

She smelled his closeness before he slid his hand under the back of her head, checking if she had cracked her head open with the fall.

"Miss, are you alright? Don't move; let me check your head before you sit up. You hit that door pretty hard. I should have opened it slowly to make sure no one was coming down the hall. I'm so sorry."

No matter how hard she tried, she couldn't speak. The familiar click of heels announced Mrs. Sorensen as she asked what all the commotion was about.

"For heaven's sake, what are you doing on the floor?" Mrs. Sorensen said in an irritated voice.

The sharpness of her tone forced her to sit up. Henry was quick to interrupt before she had a chance to answer. "This is my fault. I opened the door in front of her."

Ignoring the woman's obvious displeasure with the situation, Maggie waited for Henry to remove his hand from the back of her head.

Surprisingly, her voice didn't fail her. "Thank you; I think I'm fine." Taking a second to compose herself and pull her skirt back down over her knees, she continued in a hushed tone as she let him help her up. "I'm a little embarrassed, but I don't feel any pain."

Henry was quick to add. "I learned my lesson. No more barreling out a closed-door without being conscious of what might be on the other side. Again, I'm sorry, and I'm glad you're not hurt."

Pushing her *kapp* back in place, she glanced in Mrs. Sorensen's direction just as the woman motioned her head in the direction of the kitchen.

Making her way to the room, she sat at the small table in the corner and tried to calm herself. The peacefulness only lasted a few seconds before Mrs. Sorensen walked through the door and called her name in a sharp tone, indicating she was to follow her.

Trying to hold her head high and not let the boldness of the woman frazzle her, she dutifully followed.

"Close the door." Mrs. Sorensen grunted as she made her way to the brown leather chair that sat behind the carved mahogany desk.

Choosing to stand to take her scolding, Maggie waited for Mrs. Sorensen to begin.

"Twice in one day. I assume you're not interested in making it three?"

"No, ma'am."

Maggie stood utterly still as the older woman wrote something on the clipboard in front of her.

"I'll be leaving to run some errands and need you to work on this list while I'm gone. Mr. Waldorf and Mr. Schrock will be meeting in the dining room. Please set out drinks and be certain they're not disturbed."

Taking the clipboard, she was dismissed with a flip of Mrs. Sorensen's hand.

Once she was safely away from the office, she took in a deep breath and tried to calm her nerves. Taking a minute to get a drink of water, she stood at the sink and thought to herself. *No one has ever spoken to me in such a manner. What have I gotten myself in to?*

Picking up her list, she headed back upstairs to take inventory of the supplies in the cleaning closet. Reaching in her pocket for the master key, she hesitated when it was empty. Moving the clipboard to her other hand, she checked the other pocket and nothing. Wondering what she could have done with it, she thought. *"It must have come out when I fell in the hallway.*

Making her way back downstairs, she crawled on her hands and knees, looking under every stand and in every corner for the key. Standing and resting her hands on her hips, she said, "Where on earth could it be?"

The sound of heavy footsteps on the staircase reminded her she needed to set drinks out in the dining room. Heading back to the kitchen, she added drinks and snacks to a tray and almost dropped them as she turned to meet Henry face to face. He stood in the doorway, twirling her key on the long yellow ribbon it was attached to.

In a playful tone, he said, "I think this fell out of your pocket when I knocked you over."

Maggie sat the tray on the counter and said, "Thank goodness. I wasn't looking forward to telling Mrs. Sorensen I lost a key on my very first day."

Walking toward him, she reached out to take the key at the exact moment he pulled it back from her grasp.

"Oh no, you don't. You ran away from me at the bus station before I even caught your name, so I'm not letting you go so easily this time. We've not been formally introduced, and until we are, I'll be the holder of this key."

Smiling in her direction, he rocked the key back and forth in front of her, letting it sway from side to side without letting her catch it.

Crossing her arms over her chest and cocking her head, she asked, "You're holding me hostage for a key?"

"I guess I am if you look at it that way."

As butterflies swirled in her stomach, she hoped her voice would continue to work in her favor.

"Margaret Fisher from Tomah, Wisconsin, but I prefer Maggie."

Handing her the key, he said, "Nice to meet you, Maggie Fisher. Henry Schrock from Elkhart, Indiana."

Setting the tray on the counter, she folded her fingers around the key and placed it securely in her pocket, as she said, "Okay."

Noticing the puzzled look on his face by her silly response, she waited until he left before going back to her task.

"Okay," she mumbled under her breath. "What kind of response was that?"

Carrying the tray to the dining room, she hoped they had started their meeting and wouldn't have to endure another awkward conversation.

Trying to sit the tray down without disturbing them, she couldn't help but overhear Mr. Waldorf explain his plan to build a franchise of his bakery in Willow Springs. Hearing the rattle of paper behind her, she glanced in their direction as she left the room. Mr. Waldorf had unrolled a collection of blueprints in the center of the dining room table. Oh, how she would love to get a peek at what he had planned, but she knew better than getting in their way.

By the time she had finished everything on her list, Mrs. Sorensen made it back to the Inn and dismissed her for the day. The sun was starting to fall behind the horizon as she walked home. Dark clouds were beginning to form, and she was sure snow would fall before daylight. There was a stillness in the air, unlike the butterflies swimming around her stomach as she thought of Henry Schrock. There was something mysterious about him, unlike any other boy she had ever met. The way he carried himself reminded her of her *datt*. Strong square shoulders that made you feel safe in his presence. But it was those dark gray eyes and way too long eyelashes for a man that held the mystery.

Stomping the snow off her boots before opening the door, Maggie was greeted with the scent of cinnamon in the air as she took her coat off and hung it on the hook by the door.

"Oh, good. You're home. We've been dying to learn how your first day of work went." Lizzie said in a curious tone.

Teena pulled a pan of apple crisp from the oven and placed it in the middle of the table, as she said, "I have to know, is Mrs. Sorensen as hard to work for as all the young girls say she is?"

Maggie pulled out a chair and flopped down on it and said, "Oh, boy, is she ever. I think I've met my match with her. My family thought I was bossy, but hands down, she has me beat by a mile."

Both Teena and Lizzie pulled out a chair and sat intently, waiting for her to go into more detail.

Teena reached for the sugar bowl and stirred a heaping spoon in her tea as she said, "Tell us every detail; we want to hear it all."

Maggie wasn't much for gossiping, but she couldn't help but indulge their curiosity. For the next thirty minutes, she explained how she had been reprimanded not once but twice. And how she ended up on the floor, skirt above her knees and all. Looking back on it, she wondered how she still had a job at the end of the day.

Pushing herself away from the table, Lizzie stood and walked to the stove to stir the chicken soup and said, "I'd say you had an interesting first day."

Teena piped in as she reached for a knife to slice the loaf of bread cooling on the counter. "I want to know more about this Henry Schrock. What kind of business does he have in Willow Springs? Especially with an Englisher."

"I'm not sure, and I didn't want to be too nosy. I do know that Mr. Waldorf has something to do with the baking business, and he is looking to build something here in Willow Springs. Isn't that exciting?" Maggie asked as she picked a clump of brown sugar off the top of the apple crisp and popped it in her mouth.

Lizzie turned around and let out a small gasp and said, "Then, it's true."

"What's true?" Maggie asked.

Teena held her knife in the air and said, "Rumor has it, Mrs. Sorensen is about to sell off the land across from the Inn to a company from New York. The paper listed them as Waldorf Baking Company."

In a confused tone, Maggie asked, "Why is that a problem?"

"Because if they build here, it might put Miller's Bakery out of business. They could never compete with a professional bakery. Ezekiel and Edna count on the money they make from the tourist that stops by. If an English bakery comes to town, those tourists might be more interested in going there."

Lizzie was quick to add. "Maggie, you should know better than anyone how important cottage businesses are to the Amish. Most times, it's the only way some families can make ends meet."

"Oh my, you're right. I understand how that would be worrisome."

With a click of her tongue, Lizzie turned back around and said, "A shame for sure and certain."

Chapter 5

Blueberry Muffins

Sleep eluded Maggie as she woke long before sunrise in an unfamiliar bed, along with visions of a certain dark-haired man. No matter how hard she tried, she couldn't push the memory of him tenderly holding the back of her head and his playful smile as he swung her key in front of her face.

Getting up and tiptoeing to the kitchen, Maggie lit the oil lamp that hung above the table. The soft glow bounced shadows off the wall as the flickering wick gave her the light she needed to make a cup of tea. Hearing the mumbled voices of her aunts long after eleven the night before, she quietly fumbled around the strange kitchen, looking for everything she needed without waking them.

Adding small pieces of kindling to the firebox and lighting it, she patiently waited for the fire to heat the cast iron stove top enough to boil water. Her nightdress did little to ward off the winter chill, so she took a few minutes to go to the basement to add coal to the furnace. As she returned to the kitchen, the white porcelain teapot started to whistle softly, and she filled the waiting mug.

Carrying her cup to the round oak table, she stirred in a spoon of honey before taking a seat. Blowing over the top of the mug before taking a sip, she found herself looking forward to going to work. Not that she was excited to be at Mrs. Sorensen's beck and call, but she wanted to figure out if the rumor was true. More importantly, she wanted to know what part Henry played in Mr. Waldorf's plans.

Suddenly a longing for home forced her thoughts to her *schwesters* and how they might be handling the added responsibility of keeping the baking orders filled. By this time of the day, ten loaves of bread would be raising, and a few batches of cookies would be making their way to the oven. Mornings had always been her favorite part of the day, a time when the house was quiet and a chance to get a jump start on her baking before getting the *kinner* ready for school. No way around it, she missed digging her hands into a batch of bread dough and kneading it until it was smooth.

Looking around the small kitchen, she found a loaf of bread and helped herself to a slice. It wasn't as fluffy or as sweet as she liked, but it would fill her stomach just the same. Noticing there were only a few slices left, she found the ingredients she needed and went to work making a batch of dough before heading to work. Adding her secret ingredient, she hoped her aunts wouldn't mind if she sweetened it up a bit. Her customers in Tomah raved about her honey wheat bread, and she hoped Teena and Lizzie would like it as well. Placing the kneaded dough in a greased bowl and placing it in a warm spot near the stove, she covered it with a towel and hurried to change out of her nightgown.

~~

The sun was starting to light Willow Springs as Maggie walked the half of mile to the Apple Blossom Inn. Overnight, winter left four or five inches of heavy snow on the ground, and she took the time to stomp off the snow from her boots before she made her way through the back entrance of the Inn. Hanging her coat on the hook by the door and changing from her boots to her black shoes, Maggie tied a pink apron around her waist and went to find Mrs. Sorensen. The clock on the wall chimed seven as she made her way down the hall.

Softly knocking on the office door, she waited for Mrs. Sorensen to look up and acknowledge her before she entered.

In an agitated tone, Mrs. Sorensen said, "We have a problem. Amanda sent word she's not well and won't be coming in today. I need you to fill in for her in the kitchen. Normally she is here by six, and it's already seven. I trust you can pull something together quickly?"

Tapping the end of her pencil on the desk, Mrs. Sorensen continued, "I like to have a pot of coffee and some sort of pastry on the buffet in the dining room for those guests who rise early. Mr. Waldorf and his wife normally come down by eight and sit in the parlor to read the paper. That should be your first concern."

With a sureness in her voice, Maggie answered, "That won't be a problem."

"Good." Mrs. Sorensen answered dismissing her.

Trying to hide the smile that was making its way to her lips, Maggie turned and headed to the kitchen. Glancing at the clock once again, she noted she had fifty-five minutes, not enough time for anything that involved yeast, but enough time for muffins. Opening the refrigerator and taking inventory of what was inside, she pulled out blueberries and a carton of sour cream. Popping one of them in her mouth to check for sweetness, she pulled the rest of the ingredients from the cupboard and got to work.

After placing the filled tin in the oven, the squeak of the door announced a visitor behind her.

In an apologetic tone, Henry said, "I know it's early, but I was hoping I could get a cup of coffee. I didn't see any in the dining room and was hoping you might have some going in here."

Brushing flour from her hands, she looked toward the coffee pot on the counter and said, "Oh my, I completely forgot. Let me make it, and I'll bring you a cup as soon as it's finished."

Walking over to the restaurant-style coffee pot, she glared at its shiny buttons. Mumbling to herself, she said, "That is if I can figure this thing out. It sure is different from the percolator we use at home."

Not realizing she said it out loud, she was startled when he walked up beside her and said, "My sister runs a coffee shop back home. I can show you how it works if you want."

Without saying a word, she listened intently as he described where to add the coffee grounds, water, and what setting she needed to choose. Leaning in closer and whispering in a hushed tone, he asked, "Do you want to know the secret to good coffee?"

Tilting her head and waiting anxiously for his secret, she said, "Sure."

"It's salt."

In a questioning tone, she repeated, "Salt?"

Watching as he reached for the grinder from the counter, he turned the knob two quick times over the basket of fresh coffee grounds before sliding the basket back in its place.

Handing her the shaker, he said, "A pinch or two of salt will take the bitterness out of coffee."

Without waiting for her to answer, he turned and left the kitchen. Not moving from the counter, she watched as the hot water started to flow through the grounds and into the waiting pot below. He did it again. He left her speechless, filled her stomach with butterflies, and left her wanting to know more about what brought him here and how long he was staying.

Peeking in the glass door of the oven, she checked on the muffins before turning her attention to what she could make for breakfast by nine o'clock. That didn't leave her much time. An egg and sausage casserole and fresh fruit would have to do on such short notice.

As the last of the water filtered through the coffee grounds, she found a serving pot to fill as she waited for the muffins to finish baking. Silently hoping Henry was in the parlor or dining room, she pressed her apron out and made sure her hair was neatly confined under her *kapp.* Setting the pot on the buffet, she listened for any signs of movement in the parlor, she peered around the doorway, hoping to catch a glimpse of Henry before returning to the kitchen.

Sitting in the far corner in a wing back chair that flanked the fireplace, he sat with an open bible on his lap. His head bowed, and his eyes closed. Not wanting to disturb him, a rush of warmth filled her cheeks as she secretly glanced his way. Backing away, she bumped right into Mr. Waldorf as he came down the stairs.

Jumping as her shoulder met his extended arm, she let out a small gasp and turned around.

"Whoa girl," the older gentleman said as he reached out his hand to steady her stumble.

Embarrassed she'd been caught, she said, "I'm sorry I wasn't watching what I was doing." Making her way back to the dining room, she pointed to the coffee on the buffet and said, "I made a fresh pot, and I'll bring hot water for Mrs. Waldorf's tea in a few minutes. Muffins are in the oven, and I'll bring them out soon."

Blueberries and sugar filled her nose as she opened the oven to check on the muffins. Like always, instinctively, she knew they were ready. The sugar and butter crumble she added to the top of each muffin had nicely browned, and small bubbles of blueberry syrup made their way through the topping. "Perfect," she said to herself as she pulled the muffin tin from the oven.

Letting them sit in their tin for a few minutes, she kept busy looking for a platter to serve them on. The kitchen was stocked with plenty of serving dishes and fancy white paper lace liners to add a touch of class to the simple muffins. As she waited for the muffins to cool, she poured herself a cup of coffee, wondering if Henry's tip made a difference. Adding a splash of cream to her cup, and savoring its taste, she swirled the hot liquid around in her mouth, waiting for the bitterness. "Well, I'll be," she said out loud. "He might have something here."

Adding the muffins to the tray, she carried them to the dining room only to find Henry and Mr. Waldorf sitting at the table.

Mr. Waldorf spoke up as soon as she entered the room. "Whatever you've been baking sure smells good. You're making this old guy's stomach rumble."

"I'm sure they won't be as good as what comes from your bakery, but I hope you'll enjoy them," she said as she carried the tray to them.

"Let me be the judge of that," Mr. Waldorf said as he took a muffin from the tray. "If they're half as good as this coffee, I'll be pleased. Not sure what you did different but keep it up."

Looking over at Henry, hoping he wouldn't share their secret, he smiled and winked her way.

Holding the tray out to Henry, she waited as he took one, and watched as he held it close to his nose before taking a bite. For some reason, she held her breath, waiting for his reaction to the man-size bite.

It was Mr. Waldorf who spoke up first.

"Maggie, did you make these muffins?"

"Yes, sir. Do you not like them?" she asked nervously.

"Quite the opposite, they're good. Where did you learn to bake like this?"

Before she had a chance to answer, Mrs. Sorensen's heels alarmed her, and she turned to leave, responding to Mr. Waldorf's question over her shoulder as she left the room.

"I'm glad you're enjoying them, it's an old family recipe."

~~

By the time she finished serving breakfast and cleaned up the kitchen, Mrs. Sorensen had left a clipboard on the counter filled with her tasks for the day. Without giving her any instruction, the older woman left it, poured herself a cup of coffee, and took a muffin from the counter before returning to her office.

Drying her hands on a towel, Maggie walked over to the list and read through each item carefully. Her to-do-list was long, but hard work never scared her. Picking up the clipboard, she left the kitchen and headed to the parlor to check on the guests that gathered there.

Mrs. Waldorf was sitting in a chair near the fireplace, and Henry was adding a log to the cozy fire.

As she entered the room, Henry stood and tipped his head her way, quietly acknowledging her. Mr. Waldorf addressed her as soon as she walked into the room.

"Young lady, I have to commend you on breakfast." Patting his stomach, he continued, "I went back for thirds on those muffins. They were some of the best I've had."

Holding her clipboard tight to her chest, she tried not to smile while listening to his praise.

Changing the subject, she said, "The dining room is clean, and you and Mr. Schrock can use it as you please today."

Folding the paper he held in his hands and laying it on the coffee table in front of him, Mr. Waldorf added as he looked toward Henry. "We have much to discuss today; isn't that right, Henry?"

Turning her attention to Henry, as he moved the logs around in the fire with the iron poker, he answered in a strange tone. "I suppose we do."

Not wanting to engage with them any longer than needed, she excused herself. As she headed upstairs, she couldn't help but wonder why Henry seems so bothered by Mr. Waldorf's comment. It was clear whatever he wanted to discuss; Henry wasn't looking forward to it. Thinking back to the conversation with her aunts, she was dying to know what Mr. Waldorf's plans were. But more importantly, she wondered how Henry fit into it all. There was something about his quiet demeanor that left her wanting to know everything there was to know about him.

Chapter 6

Double Chocolate Brownies

Morning turned into late afternoon by the time Maggie completed all but one job from her list. Before she could leave for the day, she needed to go to town to pick up a few things from the Mercantile. Exchanging her pink apron for her heavy wool coat and boots, she tucked her list in her pocket and tied her bonnet over her starched white *kapp* before heading outside.

Standing on the porch, she tilted her head to the sun and took in a deep breath, letting winter fill her lungs. A strong, pungent smell filled her nose as she followed the scent to the field across the road. Two Belgium horses effortlessly pulled a manure spreader around the field, layering a fresh coat of fertilizer on top of the blanket of snow. A sudden longing for Wisconsin filled her thoughts as the sight reminded her that her *bruders* were probably doing the same thing.

Pulling her coat tighter around her middle, she headed toward the road and in the direction of town. Not exactly sure where the Mercantile was, Mrs. Sorensen assured her she couldn't miss it. She was excited about the walk and the chance to explore Willow Springs.

~~

Henry stood at the window, his back toward Mr. Waldorf as the man explained again how and why he was sure Willow Springs would be the perfect location for his new bakery. Henry was unsettled about the project and needed to talk to his *datt* before he signed any contract with the Waldorf Company. "I know you're anxious to get this contract signed, but I need to talk it over with my father first."

In an aggravated voice, Mr. Waldorf responded, "I thought you had complete control and could speak on behalf of your father. Had I known you couldn't make decisions on your own, I would have insisted your father attend this meeting."

Taken back by the man's direct tone, Henry said, "As I've said before, Schrock Construction doesn't take on a project if there's a chance an Amish business may be affected by it. I need to do my research on the area before agreeing to serve as General Contractor on your project."

Mr. Waldorf closed the folder in front of him and said, "I'm running out of time. If Schrock Construction isn't interested in this project, I'm sure I can find another construction company that is. I'll give you twenty-four hours to make your decision, and then I'll be opening the bids again."

Standing to leave the room, Henry tried to ignore the older man as he mumbled under his breath. "I should have known better than to work with an Amish Contractor."

Not sure what to make of Mr. Waldorf's comment, he turned his attention back to the window and excused himself for a breath of fresh air. Hearing the clock on the wall ring three chimes, he grabbed his coat and hat off the back of the chair and headed out the door. He had an appointment in town he didn't want to miss.

Taking the steps two at a time, Henry made his way down the front steps and around the side of the house at the same time Maggie walked from the back door. Looking toward the road, he failed to notice her as he rounded the corner, allowing her to walk smack dab into him.

Reaching out to catch her from falling as they bumped into one another, he said, "If we keep running into each other like this, one of us is going to get hurt."

Holding onto his arm as she steadied herself, she quietly thanked him.

Leaving her gloved hand on his arm longer than expected, she held his gaze as she steadied herself.

Breaking the silence, Henry asked, "Where are you off to?"

Patting the list in her pocket, she said, "To the Mercantile for a few supplies. And you?"

"I'm headed to the Sandwich Shoppe."

As they both started to walk side by side down the shoveled sidewalk, he asked, "Do you mind if I walk with you?"

Her stomach did a little flip, but she was getting used to it as it was becoming a repeat occurrence every time she was near him. Trying to sound unaffected by his closeness, all she got out was, "Sure."

They walked in silence for the first few seconds before he started to pepper her with questions.

"You never told me what brought you to Willow Springs."

There was no way she was about to tell him the real reason she was sent to Willow Springs, so it took her a few seconds to gather her thoughts and give him a reason. "I came to stay with my aunts."

As the sidewalk ended and turned into the road, they walked close to one another as they made their way into town. Hearing tires on the frozen ground as it swung out wide to pass them, Henry grabbed her arm and switched places with her on the road and said, "I'd rather be the one to get hit."

The small gesture made her feel all warm and fuzzy. Never had she had a boy, let alone a man, want to protect her in such a manner. Even though layers of wool, his touch warmed her skin long after his brief contact.

Without missing a beat, he continued, "I hear the cheese is good in Wisconsin. Is that so?"

Being careful not to slip on an icy patch in the road, she instinctively reached out and grabbed his arm to steady herself before she answered. "My *datt* and *bruders* raise dairy cows that supply milk to the cheese factory in Tomah."

"You don't say." Pausing as if he was trying to find the right words, he continued in a longing tone. "I've always wanted to farm, but it's not been in the cards for me."

Hearing the change in his voice, she looked up at him, and in a hushed tone, she asked, "Why?"

"I don't know. I guess I assume my parents expect me to work in the family business."

"Do they know you'd rather farm?"

Without answering, he walked to the side of the road and stood at the fence as he studied the way the farmer skillfully guided his team through the barren field.

"This is the piece of land Mrs. Sorensen is selling to Mr. Waldorf."

"So, it's true? He wants to build a bakery right here in Willow Springs?"

"Yep, that's his plan."

"But what about that farm and house, will he tear it down?"

"I suppose so. The land is more valuable than the barn and house, and he has no use for either of them."

With a deep sigh, he turned from the fence and made his way back to her side.

Dutifully she followed, dying to ask him more questions, but chose to keep quiet to see if he'd offer any more information freely.

Noticing he was deep in thought, they walked in silence for the next few minutes.

Henry was the first to speak. "So, tell me about yourself."

"Not too much to tell." She replied.

"I find it hard to believe you traveled over six hundred miles just to stay with your aunts. There's got to be more to the story."

Changing the subject, she asked, "Why Willow Springs?"

"Why Willow Springs, what?"

"Why is Mr. Waldorf interested in Willow Springs for his bakery?"

"Are you trying to change the subject?"

"No, I'm just curious why he wants to build a bakery here. Doesn't he know if he does it may put Millers Bakery out of business?"

Stopping in the road, he turned to face her and asked, "So, there is an Amish bakery here?"

"My aunts said Ezekiel and Edna Miller count on the money they make from their in-home bakery to support their family."

In a determined voice, he said, "I was afraid of that."

"Aunt Lizzie says if an English bakery comes to Willow Springs, many of the local businesses may suffer. The tours that visit the Millers will most likely want to go to a larger bakery, and the restaurant in town may lose their breakfast crowd. Many of the young Amish girls work at that restaurant, and they could be out of a job."

Letting what she said sink in, she waited a few seconds before she asked again. "Why Willow Springs?"

Henry flipped up his collar to ward off the wind and said, "He wants to advertise it as a destination place deep in Amish Country and pull in tourists off the Interstate."

Maggie watched her steps to be sure she didn't slip on the icy road and didn't look up as she said, "I have to side with the Millers on this one. If a new fancier bakery came to Tomah, it would hurt my business."

"Your business? You own a bakery?"

"Not really mine, but my *mamm's*."

"Well, I'll be. I guess it's the reason those muffins were so good."

Pushing her closer to the side of the road as a delivery truck slowed down and passed, he waited until its loud engine faded before he asked.

"Do you think your aunts would talk to me? I'd love to learn more about the businesses here in Willow Springs before I decide if Mr. Waldorf's project is a good fit for Schrock Construction."

"I'm sure they would. If you'd like, you could come for dinner tonight; they always make more than enough."

"That would be perfect. Thank you for the invite. What time?"

"Would six work for you?"

"I'll make it work." He said as he guided her up onto the sidewalk in front of the Sandwich Shoppe.

"I'll leave you instructions on where they live on the desk at the Inn."

"Thank you. Oh, and I'm not letting you off the hook so easy."

"What are you talking about?" She asked in a questioning tone, even though she knew what he was referring to.

"You still haven't answered my question on what brought you to Willow Springs."

Playfully she turned to leave and said over her shoulder. "It's my story, and I choose not to tell it."

Laughing at her comment, he waited until she took a few steps before shouting, "We'll see about that."

~~

Maggie couldn't wipe the smile from her face if she wanted to. The twenty-minute walk into town had been the highlight of her visit to Willow Springs thus far. From the protective way he kept her safe from the passing cars, to his concern about the Millers Bakery; he certainly was someone she found interesting.

Pulling the list from her pocket, she looked ahead, trying to locate the Mercantile. Spotting the white building trimmed in red, she picked up her pace, excited to finish work and head home in time to help Aunt Lizzie and Aunt Teena with dinner.

Walking into the older building, she stopped just inside the door and tried to acclimate herself to the market. The row of freezers to her right led to the meat counter at the back of the building. Exactly where she needed to start. A line had already formed waiting to be served by the one and only attendant behind the glass case. Looking down at her list, she decided to find the other items while waiting for the line to die down. Picking up a red handbasket, she made her way to the grocery lined shelves past the meat counter. As she walked the aisles, locating the chocolate chips Amanda needed for brownies, she walked right in the middle of a conversation.

Trying to ignore the two girls standing in front of the baking items she needed, she overheard one of the girls say, "But I don't want to meet him. He'll try to talk me into going back, and I'm not ready."

The other girl added items to her cart and said, "How do you know he'll want to take you back? Maybe he wants to make sure you are doing alright. Don't you owe it to him to at least talk to him?"

"I know him. He'll tell me how much he's missed me and how I broke my family's heart. He'll make me feel guilty for leaving, and I'm not ready to listen to all of that."

There was something strange about the conversation. The young girls faded blue jeans and hooded college sweatshirt did little to hide the fact that her pitch and tone was Pennsylvania Dutch. Trying not to be too obvious, Maggie walked around the girls excusing herself as she continued to fill her basket.

The English girl asked, "What are you afraid of?"

The girl in the sweatshirt hung her head and shuffled her feet before answering. "That I'll cave when I see him."

"I'd say if that's how you feel, you need to meet him and let your heart tell you what you need to do. It's been two years. You owe it to yourself to be sure this is what you want."

"I suppose you're right."

The English girl gave her a side hug as she said, "Go talk to him. Maybe he isn't here to take you back; maybe he just wants to check on you to make sure you are alright."

Eavesdropping wasn't something Maggie typically took part in, but there was something so familiar about the girl she couldn't pull herself away. When the two girls left, she headed back to the meat counter.

Maggie finished her shopping and found herself at the checkout counter right behind the two girls. As they finished paying for their groceries, the English girl said, "Go, I'll be at the Library. You promised to meet him, and I'm sure you'll be happy you did once you do. Don't make any speculations until you hear him out."

Maggie watched as the girl pulled her hood up over her long ponytail and pushed the door open to leave.

Intrigued by their conversation, she couldn't help but wonder if the young girl left a special someone on her *Rumshpringa.* Obviously, she jumped the fence into the English world. The sudden urge to follow her made her look both ways as she balanced the brown bag on her hip and pushed her way through the store's double doors. Not seeing any sign of her, she said a silent prayer that the young girl would find her way back to her Amish community. The English world was no place for a young girl like that to be out on her own.

Picking up her pace, she paused only for a minute to look through the big glass window of the Sandwich Shoppe. It took her only a second to recognize Henry's broad shoulders seated with his back to the window in the middle of the room. Her face warmed as she recalled their walk into town. Goosebumps started to tingle her arms but turned to ice when she recognized the girl from the Mercantile sitting directly across from him.

Chapter 7

Chocolate Cake with Peanut Butter Frosting

An afternoon that seemed so hopeful turned into an evening filled with disenchantment. Just when Maggie started to think there was something special about Henry, the reality of seeing him with the girl from the Mercantile soured her mood. She was sure both Lizzie and Teena noticed since both had been hammering her with questions.

After placing a bowl of soup in front of her, Lizzie placed both hands on her hips and said, "You might as well spill the beans and tell us what's up with the long face."

Unfolding a napkin and laying it across her lap, she said, "It's nothing."

Teena scooted her chair closer to the table as she said, "I'd say it was more than nothing by the way you've been moping around since you got home. Normally you fill us in on every detail of your day, and tonight, nothing." Reaching for a biscuit off the platter in the middle of the table, she continued, "Why don't you get it off your chest and be done with it. Stewing about whatever is bothering you will only make it worse. Sometimes all you need to do is talk about it, and it fixes itself."

Before Maggie had a chance to answer, the clock in the sitting room started to chime, and a loud knock on the front door startled all three women.

"Who could that be, and right when we were about to eat?" Lizzie said as she headed for the door.

Maggie knew who it was before the door even opened. She had completely forgotten she had invited Henry to dinner. She pushed herself away from the table and headed to the front room as Lizzie opened the door.

Looking blankly at the man standing on the porch, Lizzie asked, "What can I help you with?"

Stammering on his words, he clearly could tell the older woman wasn't expecting him. "I'm sorry, maybe I got my directions mixed up. I'm not from around here and had to ask for directions. I'm looking for the Fisher house."

"You found it. But we weren't expecting any visitors." Lizzie replied in a questioning tone.

Maggie walked up behind Lizzie and said, "I invited Mr. Schrock to dinner.

"My goodness come on in out of the cold. You're just in time and not one minute too late."

Opening the door wider and standing off to the side to let him in, Lizzie waited until he passed before giving Maggie a look of confusion.

Shooing her Aunt off with a nod of her head, she held her hands out to take his hat and coat, which she hung on the peg by the door. Giving him time to take his wet boots off before leading him to the kitchen, she was relieved Lizzie had set another place at the table.

Teena was the first to speak as she pointed to the chair, telling him to take the seat next to Maggie. "Schrock? Can't say we have any Schrocks in these parts. We have plenty of Bylers and Shetlers but no Schrocks. Where do your kin come from?"

"Elkhart, Indiana." He said as he pulled his chair out and sat down.

"Well, you don't say. Never been to those parts, but I know of one family who moved out that way and found work in a factory making campers. Do you know the one I'm talking about?"

Henry was quick to answer Teena's question. "I sure do. There are quite a few men who work in the factories in Elkhart, more factory workers than farmers these days."

Teena reached for his bowl and filled it with chicken soup as she added, "What a shame, so many families have to rely on work outside the home. I suppose farmland is hard to come by in Indiana, just like here in Pennsylvania."

Reaching out to take his bowl back, he carefully set it down and bowed his head for a few seconds before responding. "I think the younger men have gotten used to factory work more than farming."

It was Lizzie who was quick to add, "I don't understand what's going on in the world. Don't people realize children need both parents at home? A father should find a way to make a living off the land or at least close to home."

Henry picked up a biscuit and spread it with butter as he said, "I think the lure of a weekly paycheck and the lack of farmable land forces young families to make other choices. For myself, I would rather be farming than anything else, but it's not been my lot in life."

Teena put her spoon down, and without missing a beat, she said, "Did you come here to help that English fellow build a bakery? Not sure that would be the best for the Miller's."

Raising his eyebrow, he looked over at Maggie and waited a few seconds before answering. "That was the reason I was invited to dinner, even if the invitation seemed to get lost somewhere."

Maggie didn't say a word but kept on eating, pretending she didn't notice his apparent confusion.

"Just for the record, I haven't signed any contract yet. I'm still on a fact-finding mission to see if his project would be a good fit for Schrock Construction."

Teena piped in. "So, you own a construction business?"

"Not quite. I work for my *datt.* He's getting up there in age, so it works out that I handle most of the contracts when it involves travel."

Not shy about prying into Henry's personal life, Lizzie was quick to ask, "So, no special friend in the picture?"

Startled by Lizzie's question, Maggie yelped, "Aunt Lizzie!"

Taken back by her aunts' boldness, her face warmed as she glared in Lizzie's direction.

Teena grinned, cut a biscuit in half, and added, "Doesn't hurt to ask, now does it? You never know if there might be someone here in Willow Springs that could make a young man stick around a little longer."

Appalled at their embarrassing display of curiosity, Maggie hung her head, trying to shield the instant color change her face was sure to show.

Henry enjoyed the banter between the three women and took his time in answering Lizzie's question.

"Not at the moment." He said before he finished the last bite of soup at the bottom of his bowl.

Holding out her hand to take his bowl, Maggie asked, "Would you like more?"

"Sure. I've been eating at the diner the last couple of nights, and this homemade meal is hitting the spot."

Maggie took the bowl and headed to the stove. Between Lizzie's behavior and her disappointment in forgetting her invitation, she needed a minute away from the table.

Their fingers touched for a split-second as she handed him back his bowl, sending a shiver up her arm. Annoyed with her reaction to his touch, she sat in her chair, pushed her bowl aside, and decided she couldn't eat another bite.

Listening to the chatter between her aunts, Maggie watched as Henry satisfied his appetite, looking as if he was thoroughly enjoying their odd behavior. She had to admit they did have a way about them that was amusing.

Pushing his chair away from the table and leaning back, Henry patted his stomach and said, "Mighty excellent meal, ladies. That soup was great. The only thing that could make it any better would be a cup of coffee and one of Maggie's muffins."

Teena stood up, walked over to the counter, took the cover off the cake dish, and said, "We don't have any muffins, but we made this chocolate cake today. Would you like a piece?"

"Would I ever? It looks wonderful."

Maggie looked in his direction and asked, "Would you like a cup of coffee to go with it? I think I know how you like it."

"If it's not too much trouble." He said in a softer tone than he had used with Teena.

Keeping her back to the table, she tried not to read anything into the way he answered her. There was no sense getting herself all worked up again for something, or someone, who had no interest in her. She had to admit he was only there to figure out if Willow Springs was a good choice for his next construction project.

For the next hour, Lizzie and Teena answered his questions about every Amish business that may be affected by Mr. Waldorf's plans. The only thing Maggie wasn't clear on was why Mrs. Sorensen is selling the land to him in the first place. There had to be some reason she agreed to sell it without offering it to an Amish family first.

As the clock on the wall rang eight times, Henry stood, carried his cup to the sink, and headed to the door. "I best get back to the Inn and let you ladies have your evening back. Thank you again for such a fine meal and for answering my questions. I think you've helped me figure out what I already knew. Mr. Waldorf's bakery would clearly affect the lives of too many families if he built it here."

Following him to the door, Maggie reached for his coat and hat as he put his boots on.

"Do you think you really can convince him to build elsewhere?" she asked.

"I think I'll try to talk him into finding a piece of property closer to the Outlet Mall and nearer to the Interstate. He's set on that particular piece of land, but more importantly, on making it a tourist spot. This whole notion of capitalizing on the Amish Community isn't sitting well with me. I'm sure he's not about to forgo his plans even if we don't agree to take on his project. It wouldn't be hard for him to find an English Contractor who is as excited as he is to make a quick buck."

Handing him his coat, she asked, "But how can you stop him?"

"I'm not so sure I can. It's priced so high it would be hard for anyone in the community to buy it back from her."

Taking his coat from her hands, he leaned in and whispered. "Between you and me, something's not adding up. Why would a big company from New York come to Willow Springs just to build a bakery?"

Shaking her head, Maggie said in a hushed tone. "That doesn't make sense. My aunts said Mrs. Sorensen has lived here for a long time. Why would she do that to her neighbors?"

Taking his hat from her hand and moving the dark curls to the side and under his hat, he said, "Enough about that. I'm more interested in knowing what happened to my invitation."

Embarrassed that he point-blank called her out on her indiscretion, she didn't answer right away.

Looking at her feet and trying to come up with a logical answer without fibbing, she said, "It honestly slipped my mind. I'm sorry."

"I see," was all he said as he opened the door and stepped out into the cold.

~~

Not sure what to make of Maggie, Henry turned his collar up to block the wind and tried not to dwell on how his invitation got forgotten. Looking up at the sky, he waited for his eyes to adjust to the darkness before letting the moon bounce its light off the snow and guide his way back to the Inn.

The information he learned from the Fisher sisters gave him all he needed to know. There was no way Schrock Construction could take on that project, especially if it meant building on the land across from the Inn.

Mr. Waldorf wouldn't be happy, but first, he'd need to talk to his father. Next, the meeting with Bella didn't go as he planned. She changed, and any hope of bringing her home faded the minute she sat down. No matter what, he wasn't about to give up on her yet.

Turning to make his way across the street and into the warmth of the Inn, he stopped only for a moment to take one more look at the empty farmhouse. There was something so familiar about it. Could it be, all the years he dreamed of farming, this house and barn looked precisely what he envisioned in his mind?

~~

Maggie laid her hand on the cold window letting the warmth melt the frost to make a small circle on the pane. Sleep was the furthest from her mind as she recalled the look of disappointment on Henry's face. Had she imagined it, was he truly upset she had forgotten her invitation? Was she reading too much into how pleasant their afternoon walk had been? Who was the sweatshirt girl, and what hold did she have on him? Too many questions were swirling around in her head to close her eyes peacefully.

Climbing under the heavy quilt that covered her bed, she closed her eyes and put all thoughts of Henry out of her head. "Stop it," she whispered. "There I go again." Pulling the blanket over her head and squeezing her eyes tight, she tried to think of anything else. However, things like protecting her touched her in a way she'd never known before and kept him on her mind. But the fact remained the same, Henry Schrock was involved with the girl from the Sandwich Shoppe, and she'd need to push any thoughts of him far away.

Chapter 8

Banana Nut Muffins

The lamp above the table flickered as Maggie added a spoon of honey to her tea. The steam from the cup encircled the spoon as she stirred the sweetness into the mug. After a restless night, she gave up on sleep and quietly retreated to the kitchen, hoping to enjoy the peacefulness of the early morning. The pan of banana nut muffins she placed in the oven was starting to fill the house with a sweet aroma.

Her bible lay open as she tried to concentrate on the words in front of her. Taking a sip of the hot liquid, she read the verse again.

Trust in the Lord with all your heart and lean not on your own understanding; in all your ways submit to him, and he will make your paths straight.

Closing her eyes, Maggie prayed. *Heavenly, Father, I'm not sure why you sent me halfway across the country, but I trust You. I know you have a plan for me, even though I don't understand it. Please help me hear your voice and recognize the path you want me to follow. Amen.*

Just as she shut the Bible, the shuffle of feet on the polished wood floor made their way to the kitchen.

"What is that heavenly smell?" Lizzie asked as she rubbed the sleep from her eyes.

"We had a few ripe bananas on the counter, so I put them to good use," Maggie said as she got up and headed to the stove to fill a cup with hot water. Taking the cup from Maggie's hand, Lizzie said in a raspy voice. "You keep spoiling us like this, and we may never let you go back to Wisconsin."

Reaching for a potholder, Maggie opened the oven and pulled the tin from the oven sitting it down on the cast iron hot plate on the counter. It only took a few seconds for the aroma to make its way down the hallway and into Teena's room. Like at home, if she wanted to wake the house, she'd make something sweet.

"Now that's the way I always want to wake up," Teena said as she made her way into the room.

Walking to the counter, Teena leaned over the hot muffins letting the sweetness fill her nose. "Not sure I can wait until they cool."

Slapping her hand away, Maggie said, "Make yourself a cup of tea, and I'll bring you one in a few minutes. If I take them from the tin when they're hot, they'll fall apart. You can wait a few more minutes, I'm sure."

Clicking her tongue and stomping off like a child, Teena filled a mug with hot water and sat in her chair. With her back to the table, Maggie busied herself by pulling small plates from the cupboard and gathering a few cloth napkins from the drawer. Smiling to herself, Mrs. Sorensen's voice played in her head. *"It's all in the presentation."*

Unfolding a napkin and laying it across the platter, Maggie artfully arranged the muffins. Taking a small wire strainer from the drawer, she added a few teaspoons of powdered sugar and skillfully dusted the tops. Happy with the result, she carried the platter and the small plates to the table.

"Oh, my," Teena said in a cheerful voice. "Not only do we enjoy fresh muffins but served to us in such an elegant manner."

Maggie pulled her chair out and sat at the small round table, thoroughly enjoying watching her aunt's reaction to breakfast. After they all bowed their heads for a short silent prayer, Lizzie was the first to comment. "These are good, might be the best I've ever had. What on earth did you add to them to make them so moist?"

"You'll be surprised when I tell you, banana pudding. My *mamm* taught me that little trick years ago."

"You don't say. I would have never guessed." Lizzie said as she finished the muffin she was working on.

After wiping her mouth with a napkin, Teena asked, "Does Mrs. Sorensen know you're better suited for the kitchen?"

Taking a sip of her tea, Maggie said, "I'm happy to have a job, even though I'd have to admit I'd rather be baking." Pausing a moment to put her cup down, she added, "I need to be content with whatever job I have. The good Lord sent me here for a reason, and if it means I'm Mrs. Sorensen's fetch-it girl, so be it. I won't question God's plan." Standing and carrying her cup to the sink, she stated, "I best be going. I'm not sure Amanda will be back at work today."

~~

Teena waited until Maggie had her boots on and was out the door before she turned to Lizzie and said, "Did you notice how Henry held on to every word Maggie said last night?"

Lizzie reached for another muffin and added in a questioning tone. "I did, but she certainly wasn't making it easy for him. I wonder why she didn't tell us she invited him to dinner. She didn't act like she was happy he showed up."

"I know. What was that all about?"

"I'm not sure, but we might have to step in and put our matchmaking skills to work," Lizzie said as she brushed crumbs off the table and emptied them on the plate in front of her.

In a questioning voice, Teena asked, "What do you have in mind?"

"To start with, we need to make sure Henry gets an invitation to church tomorrow. It's at the Byler's, and Matthew is coming over this morning to chop wood, maybe we can have him stop by the Inn and invite him."

"What a great idea."

Gathering up their plates and carrying them to the sink, Lizzie added, "For sure and certain."

Leaning back in her chair and crossing her arms across her chest Teena said, "You know, we might just have to figure out a way for Henry Schrock to stick around for a while. If he doesn't end up taking on Mr. Waldorf's project, he may be hightailing it back to Elkhart."

Stopping at the sink and turning around to face Teena, she said, "I hadn't thought of that. How in heavens are we going to do that?"

"To begin with, we need to make sure he has someone worth sticking around for. If last night was any indication, I think that someone might be our niece. Not sure either one of them knows it yet, but I think love is in the air."

In a mischievous tone, Lizzie added, With spring around the corner, I'd say it's the perfect time to help love blossom. And the Lord knows we're good at pushing it along a bit."

Letting out a little giggle before she responded, Teena said, "We wouldn't want to let Josiah down, would we? He sent her here for one reason only, and that was to find a husband, and we need to help it along as good as we can. Don't you agree?"

"I certainly do. Our first step is for him to get rooted in the community. That shouldn't be too hard."

Standing and pushing her chair in, Teena added, "Our next step is to make him a regular guest at our table. That will keep us in the loop of his plans."

Drying her hands on a towel, Lizzie said in an excited tone. "Oh, *schwester,* I love this."

"I know, me too. I hope Matthew won't have a problem stopping by the Inn to invite Henry to church." Teena replied before leaving the room.

~~

Maggie made her way to Mrs. Sorensen's office after she was certain Amanda had the kitchen under control. Lightly knocking on the open door, Maggie waited for the older woman to look up before she entered the room.

"No need to knock child, I've been expecting you. I still haven't found someone to fill the housekeeping job, so you'll need to prepare the rooms after breakfast. I'm interviewing a girl this afternoon, and if she works out, she'll start tomorrow."

Pointing to the clipboard on the edge of the desk, Mrs. Sorensen continued, "I've detailed out what needs doing, starting with scrubbing the baseboards in the parlor. Mr. and Mrs. Waldorf typically spend the early morning in there, so find time to do that job when they are in their rooms or out for the day. I don't want you getting in the way of the guests. Is that clear?"

"It is," Maggie replied as she looked over her list.

Without looking away from the computer screen, Mrs. Sorensen asked, "Have you ever worked on a computer?"

"No."

"Well, it's about time you learned. You'll need to know how to make a reservation and check-in a guest."

The thought of learning how to use a computer made her palms sweat. She could feel her fingers tense as they held tightly to the clipboard. "Okay," was all she got out before she turned to leave the office.

Before she got out the door, Mrs. Sorensen added, "I'm running some errands this morning. I'll expect you to make sure Amanda gets breakfast on the table in time. Not so sure about that girl. I may have to replace her."

Looking up over the rim of her glasses, she asked, "I thought all Amish girls knew their way around a kitchen? This one seems more trouble than she's worth. I only hired her as a favor to her mother."

Not sure how to respond, Maggie excused herself as she said, "I'll check on things right now."

"Good, I don't want Mr. Waldorf telling me the scones are dry again. And I certainly don't want her wasting ingredients by having to remake things over and over again."

"I'll be certain Amanda has things under control," Maggie said in a determined tone.

As she left, the older woman mumbled, "I should have taken the waste from her paycheck."

Maggie was sure she wasn't meant to hear her last comment and didn't respond but went straight to the kitchen to check on breakfast.

Pushing the door open that kept the kitchen hidden from the guest dining room, Maggie was alarmed when she didn't notice anything in the works. Amanda stood at the counter reading through a recipe book. When she entered the room, Amanda greeted her with a look of confusion.

"I don't smell coffee. Mr. Waldorf will be expecting some any minute." Maggie stated.

"Oh no! I forgot," Amanda said in a wavering voice. "I got so busy trying to figure out what to bake this morning it slipped my mind. I'll start it right now."

Walking to the counter and looking at the open book, Maggie asked, "What do you have planned for this morning?"

"I haven't a clue," Amanda said as she filled the coffee basket with fresh grounds.

Before Maggie had a chance to question her further, Mrs. Sorensen pushed the door open and said, "I'm leaving now. I'll be back in a few hours. I expect you both have things under control?"

"We do," Maggie said, trying to act as if things were going smoothly.

"Good, see to it."

Maggie waited until she was sure the back door open and closed before asking, "What do you mean you haven't a clue? You should have had something in the oven an hour ago."

"I know, well, really, I don't know. I'm no good in the kitchen, but I need this job. My family depends on my paycheck."

Closing the cookbooks in front of her, Maggie said, "No one said you're going to lose your job; we'll figure it out. I have an idea."

In a calm voice, Amanda asked, "What can I make quick and easy?"

Without missing a beat, Maggie picked up her clipboard and looked over the list for something she could send the girl to do while she made breakfast.

"How are your cleaning skills?"

Taking a deep breath and blowing it out before she responded, she said, "Oh, thank the Lord. I can handle the cleaning. Please give me anything but making breakfast."

Pointing to the supply closet, Maggie said, "You'll find a bucket and a sponge in that closet. The baseboards in the front room need wiped down. If you can take care of that job before the guests start coming downstairs, I'll start breakfast."

The relief on Amanda's face showed long before she wrapped her arms around Maggie and gave her a quick hug as she said, "I'll get right on it."

Glancing around the kitchen trying to come up with a plan, she noticed Amanda had forgotten to turn the coffee pot on after she filled the basket with coffee grounds. Pulling the basket out and adding the pinch of salt as Henry had shown her, she flipped the switch on and headed to the pantry.

Wishing she could bake a batch of muffins, she decided she couldn't serve them two days in a row. Pulling everything from the pantry she needed to make a quick coffee cake, she looked at the clock to make sure she had enough time for its twenty-minute bake time.

"I'm cutting it close," she whispered to herself as she greased and floured a cake pan. She knew if she could get something sweet in the dining room to hold the guests over, they wouldn't mind if breakfast was a few minutes late.

Within a few seconds of the coffee pot beeping, the kitchen door opened, and Henry stood holding an empty cup out to her.

"Can I get the first cup?" He asked as he moved in the direction of the counter.

Taking the cup from his hand before he had a chance to make it across the room, Maggie said, "I'm sorry I haven't had a chance to fill the carafe yet. Let me do that for you."

With her back to him, she filled his cup and added cream and sugar before handing it back. Surprised he settled at the island in the middle of the room, she set the cup in front of him and got back to work creaming butter for her coffee cake. Trying not to let his presence rattle her, she enjoyed watching him as he took a long sip of the hot liquid.

"You remembered the salt?" He asked in a pleasing tone.

"I did."

Looking around the kitchen, he asked, "Are you filling in for the cook again?"

"I guess you could say that. She got a little behind this morning, so I'm helping out." Changing the subject, she asked, "Are you always up this early?"

"Habit, I guess. I learned if I wanted to be my *mamm's* taste-tester, I needed to be in the kitchen before anyone else."

Without missing a beat in pouring the batter in the cake pan and sprinkling the strudel mixture on top, she carried the pan to the oven and glanced at the clock to check the time. Turning back toward the island and wiping her hands on her apron, she smiled as he licked the spoon she used to mix the cake batter.

Acting as if he had his hand in the cookie jar, he said in an apologetic tone. "I guess old habits are hard to break."

Before she had a chance to respond, Amanda made her way through the kitchen door holding a bucket in one hand and a sponge in the other.

Heading toward the counter where Maggie's clipboard sat, she exclaimed, "The baseboards are done. What's next?"

Maggie walked to the counter to look over the list as Henry quietly excused himself from the kitchen. A sense of warmth filled her cheeks at their brief conversation. It only lasted a second before she reminded herself, he was just friendly, and she needed to chase any notion of anything more from her head.

Chapter 9

Coffee Cake

Mr. Waldorf tapped his pencil on the table as he sat patiently, listening to Henry explain his reasoning for not wanting to sign the contract.

"You have to understand my position. As a businessman, I take into account how our projects would affect others. If I agree to help you build a bakery right here, a family's livelihood would be greatly affected. In my right mind, I can't be responsible for that, and my father agrees."

Clearing his throat, Mr. Waldorf replied, "You've put me in quite a spot."

Closing the folder in front of him harshly, Mr. Waldorf stood and rested his hands on the table and said, "My investors aren't going to be happy."

Reaching for the blueprints and rolling them up to slide them in their cardboard sleeve, he continued, "There's more at stake here than a few Amish businesses. You have no idea what economic impact this project would have on this town."

Henry stood and walked to the window that overlooked the farmland across the street. "I understand the predicament you're in, but there are other options."

In a stern voice, Mr. Waldorf responded, "There is, and I've already been in contact with another contractor from Pittsburgh. Unfortunately, he can't take on another project until later this year. My partners are looking to get this underway immediately."

In the back of Henry's mind, he thanked the Lord that Mr. Waldorf was running into so many obstacles. He had plans of his own, and they all centered around not using that land for what Mr. Waldorf intended.

Turning from the window, Henry stood still as the balding man busied himself by putting papers back in his briefcase as he said, "I knew you probably weren't going to sign, so I even went as far as contacting a few other Amish builders in the area, and they all gave me the same runaround. They wouldn't even consider building here if my plans meant someone might go out of business. Don't you people know this is business and nothing else?"

Not wanting to play into Mr. Waldorf's evident frustration, Henry said in a quiet and assuring tone. "I do understand, and I have a plan. Will you hear me out?"

Leaning back in his chair and crossing his arms over his chest, he said, "There isn't any other option. That land is the only choice. My partners already started the ball rolling on Phase Two."

"What's Phase Two?" Henry asked.

Standing to leave, Mr. Waldorf said in a huff. "All you need to concern yourself with is this isn't over, and it'll be on your head if it falls through."

~~

After breakfast had been served and the dining room put back in order, Maggie took her clipboard and started to work on the jobs Mrs. Sorensen had detailed out for her. Amanda had completed most of the downstairs cleaning duties while she made breakfast, and all that was left were the rooms upstairs. Walking through the parlor, Mrs. Waldorf sat near the fire, sipping a cup of tea.

"Good morning Maggie. The coffee cake you made this morning was wonderful. I'll be sure to tell Mrs. Sorensen how much I enjoyed it."

Letting out a small gasp, it only took Mrs. Waldorf a second to comment on her reaction.

"What is it?"

Maggie tried to think of an answer and quick. How could she explain that she had filled in for Amanda?

Maggie said in a hushed tone. "Not that I don't want you to tell her you enjoyed it; it's just that my job is not to cook breakfast; it's Amanda's. I was helping her out this morning, and if Mrs. Sorensen finds out we switched jobs, she might not be too happy."

"Have you thought about telling Mrs. Sorensen about your baking skills?"

"No, Ma'am."

Looking around to be certain no one was in earshot Mrs. Waldorf whispered, "I'd say she isn't using either of you to your best ability. I saw Amanda in here washing baseboards this morning; she was humming a tune, enjoying herself." Reaching up and patting the back of Maggie's hand, she said, "Your secret is safe with me."

Maggie laid her free hand over the older woman's silky knuckles, lightly squeezed them, and said, "Thank you."

Maggie didn't like asking Mrs. Waldorf to keep their secret, but at this point, neither one of them could take a chance of her finding out what they had done. Regardless, if she didn't like deceiving the woman, she'd help Amanda in the kitchen without actually doing her job one way or another.

Rounding the corner as she started up the stairs, she overheard Mr. Waldorf's gruff voice say. "Don't you people know this is business and nothing else?" Stopping on the first step, she listened as Henry said, "I do understand, and I have a plan." When she didn't hear anything more but the shuffling of papers, she continued up the stairs.

For the next couple of hours, as she changed linens and cleaned bathrooms, Henry's words played over in her head. What on earth could he be talking about, and what plan would there be but to find a way for Mr. Waldorf to build his bakery elsewhere.

As the grandfather clock in the front room rang two, the door alarm chimed, indicating someone had entered through the double doors. Mrs. Sorensen would use the employee entrance, so it must be a new check-in. Removing her rubber gloves and smoothing her pink apron, she headed down the stairs to greet the new arrival. Just as she made it to the bottom of the stairs, Mrs. Waldorf turned her way.

"There you are. This young girl says she has an appointment with Mrs. Sorensen. I was coming to look for you."

Maggie recognized the girl from the Mercantile instantly.

"Thank you; I'll show her to Mrs. Sorensen's office."

Turning her attention to the girl, she asked in a pleasant tone. "I take it you're the person she's interviewing for the cleaning position?"

In a nervous voice, the girl answered, "I am."

Leading her back to Mrs. Sorensen's office, Maggie said, "Be yourself and answer her questions honestly, and you'll do fine. By the way, my name is Maggie."

"Thank you, Maggie, I'm Bella Fleming."

As they made it to the office, Mrs. Sorensen came in the back door struggling with a few packages and a bundle of mail. Maggie ran to her aid and emptied her hands as she introduced Bella.

"This is Bella, your two o'clock interview."

In a harsh tone, Mrs. Sorensen pointed to her office door. "Go take a seat, and I'll be right in."

Standing behind the older woman as she took her boots off and replaced them with her shiny black leather heels, Maggie gave a sympathetic smile in Bella's direction, hoping to soften Mrs. Sorensen's blow.

"The weather is awful out there. The snow is blowing so hard I had to drive through whiteouts most of the way back from Grove City." Taking her coat off and laying it on top of the packages Maggie had already piled in her arms, she said, "Take those to my room and hang my coat in the closet."

"Yes, Ma'am."

Struggling to open the door to Mrs. Sorensen's private space, she jumped when Henry's arm reached around her and turned the handle.

"It looks like you could use a hand. Here, let me take some."

"Thanks, they were heavier than they looked," Maggie said as she gladly let him take the packages from her arms.

Pointing to the bed, she hung the coat and shooed him back out the door. There was no way she wanted Mrs. Sorensen to know Henry helped her.

Walking in front of him, she pushed open the kitchen door, not expecting him to follow. Surprised that he had, she turned and asked. "Can I get you anything?"

"I need to talk to your aunts again. Do you think they'd mind if I came by tomorrow?"

In a curious tone, she said, "It's a church Sunday, but you're more than welcome to stop by in the afternoon if you want."

Taking a seat at the island, he said, "Matthew Byler stopped by and invited me. Not sure how he knew I was here. I guess word travels as fast here as it does in Elkhart. No one ever stays a stranger for long."

Looking his way, Maggie said in a nervous tone, "It will be my first time as well."

Leaning in a little closer than she was comfortable with, he whispered, "Good, then we can be strangers together."

In an instant, heat rose to her face, as she remembered Bella. Before she had a chance to respond, he left her standing in the kitchen, wondering why she hung on to his every word.

Bella passed the kitchen door as she tried to ignore the butterflies in her stomach and asked, "So, how did it go?"

"Good, I start on Monday."

"Great, then I'll see you then."

She wondered if she should ask Bella about Henry. Was it possible he was playing both sides of the fence? Or was she reading more into his unmistakable charm?

~~

Taking a phone message back to Mrs. Sorensen, she stopped at the door when she realized Mr. Waldorf was with her. Not wanting to disturb her, she walked past the open door and took a seat on the bench by the back door.

From where she sat, the long corridor gave her the perfect view of Henry and Bella as they stood in the entryway. Watching as their quiet voices and closeness made it evident they knew each other personally. She couldn't help but think only a couple who'd spent a great deal of time together would look so comfortable. A lump lodged in f her throat as Henry wrapped his arm around the girl and pulled her in for a hug. She could hardly breathe.

Her gaze only broke when Mr. Waldorf raised his voice.

"It's a huge problem, and if we don't figure it out quickly, you can kiss this project goodbye."

~~

Watching as Mr. Waldorf left Mrs. Sorensen's office, she couldn't help but wonder how her boss fit into Mr. Waldorf's plans.

Snapping her fingers and pointing toward the hall, Maggie instinctively followed Mrs. Sorensen's lead as she headed to the check-in counter.

Without so much as an explanation, Maggie listened intently as Mrs. Sorensen explained how to check a guest in. Trying to keep track of the steps, she reached for a pad and pencil and started to write down the instructions.

Shaking her head and curling her eyebrow, Mrs. Sorensen said, "It's not that hard; there's no point in taking notes."

Without realizing she had spoken it out loud, Maggie replied in a sharp tone. "Well, this is the way I need to learn."

Stopping and cocking her head in Maggie's direction, she asked in a questioning voice. "Excuse me?"

Between watching Henry with Bella and trying to comprehend Mrs. Sorensen's instructions, her shoulders tensed when she realized she had spoken disrespectfully.

"Are you sure I'm the right person for this job?"

Without missing a beat, Mrs. Sorensen responded, "At the moment, you're all I have."

Confused by the woman's comment, she didn't try to figure it out as she continued to explain the ins and outs of the software, then she moved onto the telephone system. In a sharp tone, the woman asked, "You do know how to use a phone, right?"

Startled, Maggie answered, "Of course."

Closing the lid to the laptop and picking up her clipboard Mrs. Sorensen said, "Bring your notes; I have a few other things to go over with you."

Dutifully following the woman to the pantry, she listened as she explained where and how to order supplies, and what days of the week flowers were delivered. Making their way back to the office, Maggie sat in the chair Mrs. Sorensen pointed to as they entered the room.

"Look, I know I've thrown a lot at you in the past week, but I'm confident you can handle it. I've hired the new girl to start cleaning Monday, and I'll leave it to you to show her what she needs to do."

Pushing the pad across the desk in front of her, she added, "I am leaving tomorrow for Pittsburgh. Here is the number you can reach me at if you need to ask any questions. Anything you need from the Mercantile, charge to my account."

With a blank stare, Maggie was unsure what to make of everything she said. Trying to keep her voice from shaking, she asked, "What do you mean you're leaving? I barely know my way around. I'm not so sure about all of this."

In a softer tone, the woman said, "I'm confident you'll do fine. I see something in you that perhaps you don't see in yourself. You can manage things, I'm sure."

Unsure of what to make of the woman's comment, she took in a deep breath and tried to process everything.

"One last thing. I have hired a woman to come and take care of the guests tomorrow on your day off. Amanda will need to prepare an extra meal today that can easily be heated up and served for breakfast."

Tapping her pencil on the desk, she added, "I'm still not sure about that one. She doesn't seem too confident in the kitchen, but she'll have to do for now. "

Pushing her chair back away from her desk, she asked, "Do you have any questions?"

A million thoughts were spinning around her head, but not one audible question would come to mind at that exact moment. "No, I don't think so."

"Good, then I'll leave this with you, and I'll be in my room the rest of the day should you need me."

Taking the keys from the woman's outreached hands, she asked, "Why do I need the keys to your office and your room?"

Walking around the desk and out the door, the woman said in an alarmingly quiet tone. "Just in case."

Not moving from her spot in the smooth brown leather chair, Maggie closed her eyes and rubbed her fingers and thumb across her forehead, trying to make sense of what happened. How on earth did Mrs. Sorensen think she had the skills needed to run the Apple Blossom Inn?

Chapter 10

Apple Filled Moon Pies

After letting her aunts off at the basement door, Maggie pulled the buggy behind the barn. As she climbed down from the seat, she handed the reins off to the waiting boy who would unhitch it, mark their carriage, and take the horse to the barn.

Taking her time to make it to the front of the Byler house, she tried to calm her anxiety about the strange surroundings. There was nothing more she wanted then to be back home in Tomah. She missed her family, and more than anything else, she missed the familiarity of her community.

Watching as the women made their way to the basement, she stayed hidden behind the black church wagon parked on the side of the house. Void of benches and boxes of hymnals, the cart made the perfect cover. Taking in a deep breath to give herself the push she needed to proceed, she headed toward the door.

Lizzie stood holding the basement door open as she said, "Maggie, there you are. We wanted to introduce you to some of our friends. Quick come inside out of the cold."

Maggie kicked the snow off her boots and untied her black bonnet as she came through the door. As she let her eyes adjust to the room, she unfastened her coat and slipped it off while Lizzie began her introductions.

"This is Emma, Anna, and Rebecca Byler. Anna and Rebecca are twins, but you'd never guess it since they don't look a thing alike. They are Jacob Byler's daughters." Softening her tone, Lizzie continued, They lost their sweet *mamm* a few weeks ago."

The youngest of the three, Emma spoke up, "Welcome, Maggie. We're glad you've joined us today. How about you sit with us? You're about Anna and Rebecca's age, so you can file in line behind them. Your aunts tell us you are from Tomah, Wisconsin. I've never been any further than Sugarcreek, Ohio. We can't wait to hear all about Wisconsin and your family."

The tension in Maggie's shoulders instantly disappeared with Emma's warm welcome.

Moving to the side, Maggie waited as the older women fell into line, oldest to youngest, and made their way up the steps. Finding her place behind the Byler twins, she climbed the steps that led to the kitchen. Bean soup and freshly baked bread filled her nose as she walked through the kitchen and into the sitting room. Neatly lined pine benches furnished the room as the women walked around them, slowing and solemnly taking their place. Removing the black leather-bound Ausbund Hymnal from the seat and placing it on their lap, each woman stayed quiet as the procession continued. The ministers made their way around the room, acknowledging each woman as they passed and preparing them for the three-hour service.

From where Maggie sat, she could see out the front window as each man removed his hat and left it on the bench by the door. The men filled in from oldest to youngest, each with the same look of calmness and seriousness. A sense of comfort filled her as she thought it was a time for deep reflection and honor God, no matter where she was.

Laying her hand on her stomach, hoping to calm the rumbling, she regretted not eating breakfast. Anna looked toward her, smiled, and reached in her purse to pull out a red and white peppermint. Silently mouthing the word *"denki,"* she unwrapped the candy quietly.

After placing the round candy in her mouth, she lifted her head to find Henry looking back at her. When she caught his eye, he winked and nodded in recognition, making her gasp, lodging the mint candy in her throat. Coughing loud enough that every eye in the room looked her way, Emma slapped her back, sending the hard candy across the wooden floor. Heat rose in her cheeks as she excused herself and headed to the other room.

Alone in the kitchen, she took time to soothe her cough and push the wink out of her mind. Leaning on the counter, she shook her head and thought to herself. *They must do things differently in Elkhart.* His boldness was like nothing she'd experienced. She prayed no one else in the room had witnessed it.

As she walked back in, harmonious voices filled the room and gave her the cover she needed to find her way back to her seat. Making her way past the men lined up against the back wall, she was startled when Henry leaned forward and whispered, "sorry," as she passed.

Without saying a word, she made her way to the middle aisle and back to her seat. Her stomach flipped as his eyes burned a hole in the back of her starched white kapp. Thank goodness he was behind her, and she wouldn't have to look his way. As hard as she tried to listen to each of the three ministers, it was only the last sermon that made it anywhere into her mind. Hearing the Bishop recite a popular verse, she repeated it quietly in her head.

"For those who live according to the flesh set their minds on the things of the flesh, but those who live according to the Spirit set their minds on things of the Spirit."

A lump formed in the back of her throat, and she was sure it was a message sent from God. Ashamed she'd spent two and a half hours thinking of nothing but the dark curls that lay plastered to Henry Schrock's forehead. Determined to push all thoughts of him from her mind, she bowed her head and silently repented for the fleshly thoughts that had consumed her.

Anna tapped her arm, forcing her to turn in her seat and drop to her knees, asking God again to forgive her for being so self-consumed. With eyes closed tight, pools of moisture formed in the corners as she let the final words of the Bishop penetrate her thoughts. "*Heavenly Father, we bless Your holy name. We give You all the praise and glory and ask you to cleanse our minds of all worldly desires as we leave this place. Deliver us from evil and protect us from his deceitful lies. We ask all of these things in Jesus' name. Amen.*

Not wanting to lift her head from her folded hands, she willed herself to stand, along with Anna and Emma. She had much to be thankful for, and most of it had nothing to do with Henry Schrock. With a new sense of determination, she wasn't going to let her *datt's* foolish notion of finding a husband monopolize her thoughts again, or so she thought.

Anna was the first to speak as everyone gathered their things from under the bench. "Maggie, come help us in the kitchen, and we'll introduce you to the others."

Without saying a word, Maggie followed Anna and Rebecca as they made their way to the center aisle and around the back of the room. Men were already converting benches to tables as Maggie stepped out of their way and straight into Henry's path.

Refusing to acknowledge him, she lowered her head, ignoring his stance. Making it obvious, he waited until both girls passed before he put his foot into the walkway, forcing her to stop.

With a smug smile on his face, he whispered, "You didn't forget my invitation today, did you?"

The little hairs came to life on the back of her neck, and she answered through clenched teeth, "no."

Without giving him a chance to say another word, she stepped over his foot and headed to the kitchen.

~~

Standing in the doorway, trying to figure out where she could be the most help, she followed Anna's voice. "Maggie, over here, you can help us put the moon pies out."

Wasting no time in getting her hands busy, she nodded her head in acknowledgment to the girls' Anna was introducing her to.

"Maggie, this is Katie Yoder and Sarah Mast. Sarah's family owns the sawmill, and Katie's owns Strawberry Acres. We love June around here when their strawberries are as sweet as sugar. If you're still here this summer, we all get together to make strawberry jam that Rebecca and I sell at the Farmers Market." Without taking a breath, Anna excitedly continued, "We have the best fun getting together for a work frolic. Katie's *Mamm* lets us use her kitchen, and we spend the whole day together, just the five of us."

Emma handed Katie a full tray to take out to the serving table, as she said. "We hope by the time strawberry season starts we'll be able to use our new kitchen. Katie's *Datt* is trying to get permission from the Bishop to let Katie and I start a bakery at Strawberry Acres."

Maggie took an empty tray from the counter and started to fill it with more moon pies but stopped in mid-air when she heard the word 'bakery.'

"Bakery? Another one? I thought the Millers had a bakery. Can Willow Springs support two?" Maggie asked.

Katie stopped in the doorway with a full tray in her hands and commented in a concerned tone. "*Datt* thinks the Bishop is pondering that very notion. Our only hope is that since their farm is on the west side and ours is on the east, it won't affect their sales."

Maggie's first thought was she needed to tell Henry about the girls' plan. Wondering if she should say anything to Emma and Katie about Mr. Waldorf, she decided it was best to keep what she knew to herself. Remembering she saw the sign to Yoder's Strawberry Acres on her way into town, she knew Mr. Waldorf's plans would inevitably affect them. Even though she didn't relish the thought of having a lengthy conversation with Henry, she knew they needed to find a way to stop Mr. Waldorf.

Carrying a tray of apple-filled pies to the front room, Maggie looked around, hoping to catch Henry's attention. After finding a spot for the tray, Maggie scanned the room until she stopped on Henry, who sat alone across the room. Picking up a pitcher of water, she filled his glass and whispered, "I need to talk to you."

Slowly tilting his head in her direction, he said, "I was starting to think you'd like to do anything but that."

In a dismissing tone, she said, "It's not what you think. I need to talk to you about Mr. Waldorf's plans. I've learned something that you need to know."

Before he had a chance to answer, men filled the surrounding spots, putting a halt to their brief conversation. She quietly filled the remaining glasses until her pitcher was empty.

In the kitchen, Sarah and Rebecca stood at the counter, cutting bread as Emma and Katie filled small dishes with apple butter and jam. As Emma pulled a stack of bowls from the cupboard, a few recipe cards fell to the floor. Maggie stooped to pick them up and handed them to Emma after she set the dishes safely on the counter. Emma stood and looked intently at the handwriting on the cards and traced her fingers across the cards in a longing manner. Maggie instantly knew what they were long before Emma said a word.

Maggie's heart filled with compassion as pools of tears filled Emma's eyes and waited tenderly as the girl processed what she held.

Anna wrapped her arm around Emma's shoulder and said, "It's the little things like this that keep happening that remind us that *Mamm* is with us."

Maggie remembered the pain and how long it took for her to be at peace with her own mother's passing. Trying to find the right words, she waited a few moments before walking closer to say. "It's going to take a long time for the hurt to ease, and some days you'll feel like it will never go away."

Waiting for Emma to wipe her eyes on the back of her hand Maggie continued. "On those days, you have to permit yourself to grieve. I don't know if it will help, but when I didn't feel like I could do another day, I looked for something that reminded me of her."

"You lost your *mamm* too?" Anna asked.

"I did. Two years ago." Maggie answered. "There were many days I spent rocking in her chair or wrapping myself in her sweater. Or, in this case, I'd be making whatever was on those recipe cards. God doesn't want us to forget our loved ones; that is why He gave us memories."

Emma reached out and squeezed Maggie's hand and said, "Thank you, we all needed to hear that. This week has been extremely hard. Maybe God sent you to Willow Springs so that you could help us get through this."

Trying to lighten the mood, Maggie giggled before she said, "I would love to say that was my only purpose in coming here, but my family would beg to differ."

In a questioning tone, Anna asked, "Something you'd care to share with us?"

Picking up a plate of sliced bread off the counter, Rebecca added in a harsh tone. "It's going to have to wait; this food needs out to the table before Katie's *Mamm,* and the others get after us."

Anna patted Maggie's arm as she said, "Don't mind her, she can be a bit snippy, but it's how she deals with things. We cry, she gets bossy."

Maggie smiled before adding, "I've been called a little bossy myself, so I completely understand."

Chapter 11

Cherry Bars

Pulling the brown-topped buggy around to the front of the Byler house, Maggie stepped down and hooked the reins around the hitching post. Waiting for Lizzie and Teena to say their goodbyes, it was easy to see why they had so many friends. Helping each of them up into the waiting buggy, Maggie handed Lizzie the reins, as Teena asked, "Are you sure you know the way back, it's a couple of miles you know?"

"I'm pretty sure. I take a right on Willow Bridge Road and then a right on Main Street Extension, correct?"

"You got it," Teena answered.

With the click of her tongue and a wink in Teena's direction, Lizzie instructed the horse to back up and added, "Don't forget Henry is coming over this afternoon. Maybe you'll meet him along the way."

Looking around to be certain he wasn't close, she said, "I didn't forget. I'll be home shortly."

Tying her bonnet tighter and pulling the blue scarf from her pocket, Maggie looped it around her neck and headed toward the road. The fresh air was what she needed to clear her head.

~~

Standing in the shadow of the barn's open door, Henry watched Maggie as she helped her aunts settle in their buggy. He wasn't sure why Lizzie made a point to let him know she was walking home, but he was glad he had her on his side. He certainly wasn't making any points with her on his own.

He was confused by her sudden change in attitude since they walked into town the other day. For the life of him, he couldn't figure it out. Thinking out loud, he said, "*Women. I'll never understand them.*"

Walking up beside him and placing his black-rimmed hat on his head Matthew said, "I'm with you there. I've stopped trying to figure them out." Pausing to pull his collar up, he asked, "Which one has you scratching your head?"

Nodding his head in the direction of the front porch, Henry said, "That one."

"The Fisher *schwester's* niece? I hear she's working at the Apple Blossom Inn."

"That would be Maggie Fisher. How about you?"

Taking a step out of the door, Matthew said in a hushed tone and over his shoulder. "Sarah Mast, the tall one in that group of girls."

Watching Maggie out of the corner of his eye, she started to walk toward the road, and he quickly excused himself.

"Hey, thanks for inviting me today."

Matthew extended his hand and said, "I hope you stick around for a while. If you need a friendly diversion, my door is always open. Or at least you'll find me here in the barn."

Henry pulled his hat tighter on his head and said as he walked in Maggie's direction. "I might take you up on that."

~~

Maggie barely made it to the end of the driveway before she was interrupted with a voice behind her. "Maggie, wait."

Her heart fluttered with the familiar sound, but it turned to frustration as she whispered, "Oh, help!"

Not stopping, she kept on walking, knowing he'd catch up to her no matter if she wanted him to or not.

Jogging up beside her, he slowed his pace to keep in step with her smaller strides. "Where are you going? Isn't your house in the other direction?"

"If you must know, I wanted to take the long way home to have time to think."

Ignoring the sharpness in her voice, he said, "You said you wanted to talk."

Letting silence fall between them, Maggie calmed her annoyance with his intrusion as they maneuvered the snow-covered road.

Breaking the stillness between them, Henry asked, "The men were talking about Jacob Byler's wife. Did you know she passed six weeks ago?"

"Yes, I met his daughters today. I know how hard it is to lose a mother and then to have to host church so soon, I'm sure it was hard on them."

Pulling away as he pushed her to the side of the road, she snapped. "You've got to stop touching me. It isn't proper."

Taken back by her tone, he threw his hands in the air and said, "Whoa, I was only trying to keep you from being run over."

Heaviness filled the air as they walked in silence. Little did Henry know his very touch sent shivers down her back and made her think of things any respectable young Amish woman should not be thinking. If she was going to take anything from the sermon to heart, she had to lay some ground rules. And the first being no touching.

Henry stopped in the road and waited for Maggie to notice before he hollered.

"Look, I don't know what I did to upset you, but if you'd like to get it out in the open, maybe we can start over."

Stopping in the middle of the road and turning in his direction, she said, "You beat all, Henry Schrock, if you don't know, I'm not telling you. All I'm going to say is I'm not playing your games so you can stop with the sweet talk and the winking from across the room."

Taking his hat off and pushing his bangs back underneath before responding, he said in a confused tone. "Okay, I'm not sure where that came from."

Embarrassed, she realized she might have overreacted. "Look, I'm sorry. I know we barely know one another. I guess I assumed ...it doesn't matter."

Waiting until he caught up to her, she quickly changed the subject. "Emma Byler and Katie Yoder are planning on opening a bakery at Yoder's Strawberry Acres this summer."

Stopping in the middle of the road and turning in her direction, he said, "Another bakery?"

With a sense of concern in his voice, he said, "This certainly complicates things even more."

"Why do you think Mrs. Sorensen is selling him that property?" She asked.

"I've been trying to figure that out myself. From all I've learned, she held on to it for years, keeping the price so high no one could afford it. Why she is selling it to George Waldorf is beyond me."

Remembering she saw Mr. Waldorf in Mrs. Sorensen's office, she said in an excited tone. "Wait a minute. I saw Mr. Waldorf talking to Mrs. Sorensen yesterday. He was upset about something and left her office in a huff. Whatever it was, she was in a fouler than normal mood afterward."

Rubbing his chin with his gloved hand, Henry said, "Interesting. You know he slipped up and said something about a Phase 2. When I questioned him about it, he changed the subject."

"What do you think he's talking about?" Maggie asked.

"I have no idea, but I think we need to dig a little deeper and find out who Mr. Waldorf has backing this project. That might tell us why he's so adamant in building here."

Walking in silence for a few seconds, Maggie momentarily forgot her aggravation with him, that was until he said, "So, I hear you're training Bella tomorrow."

Just hearing her name roll off his lips made her stomach churn. The tenderness in his voice told her all she needed to know. As they walked, a little voice in the back of her head whispered, *You're jealous.*

Without realizing she hadn't answered him, he continued to talk. "She's a hard worker, and she'll do fine."

Waiting for an answer, he turned and looked her way when she didn't respond. "Maggie, did you hear me?"

"I did, I'm sorry... I was thinking about something else."

As they walked inside the covered bridge over Willow Creek, Henry marveled at the construction of the wood covered bridge.

"Do you know, this bridge was constructed in 1889, and is built on a stone foundation, supported by steel girders that are a hundred and twenty-one feet long?"

In an amused tone, she answered, "I can honestly say I had no idea. But I can tell you know a lot about it."

"Only what I read in a brochure at the Inn. I've wanted to see it up close."

Pointing overhead, he said, "Those are Burr Arch trusses."

She couldn't help but smile at his fascination with the bridge. Walking on ahead, she let the longing thoughts creep back into her head, but for only a split-second before she chased them away like a fly on a pie.

"We best keep walking," she hollered over her shoulder. "If I know my aunts, they already have snacks and coffee waiting on the table."

Taking a couple of long strides to catch up, he asked, "Would those snacks be anything you made? My stomach is learning to have a real fondness for your baking."

"You'll have to wait and see," she said in a playful tone.

Biting her bottom lip as soon as the words left her mouth, she thought to herself. *Oh my, I'm as bad as he is.*

As they exited the covered bridge, Henry pointed to the clouds and said, "Looks like a storm is rolling in. I read we're supposed to get hit hard this week. According to the paper, this is the last sunshine we'll enjoy for most of the week."

Maggie looked in the direction he motioned and said, "We had two people cancel their reservations yesterday because of it. I can't say I'm too upset about that since Mrs. Sorensen will be out of town."

Henry stopped on the side of the road to retie his boot and said, "Do you think she needs the money?"

"I wondered that too," Maggie said as she stopped to wait for him to finish. In a fretful voice, she said, "I have a notion, Mrs. Sorensen's trip to Pittsburgh has something to do with Mr. Waldorf's visit to her office."

Henry stood and walked up beside her and said, "All I know is I've seen it happen before. A big company like this comes into a small town and does more harm than good."

For the next twenty minutes, they watched as the bright sky slowly turned gray as they made their way back. Catching a glimpse of the blue door and the porch through the trees, Maggie said, "See what I mean? Lizzie's on the porch watching for us."

Waving as they made their way up the sidewalk Lizzie hollered. "We were starting to worry you might have taken a wrong turn somewhere."

Teena met them at the door with her hand extended, taking their coats, as she said, "Oh good, Henry, you made it too. Perfect timing."

Lizzie rolled her eyes over the top of her glasses and winked in Henry's direction as he hung his hat on the peg by the door and took off his boots.

Teena walked ahead of them and said, "Come, we have the coffee on, and we made a batch of Maggie's Cherry Bars."

"I had a big lunch, but I'm not one to turn down an afternoon snack."

Watching as Teena and Lizzie found a place at the table, Maggie went ahead and filled each cup before taking a seat of her own. Pushing the creamer toward Henry, he nodded and stirred in enough to color the dark liquid. Wrapping his hands around the mug, he took a sip and said, "This hits the spot. Nothing like a good cup of coffee on a chilly day."

Teena leaned in and said in a cheerful voice. "Do you like it? Maggie taught us a little trick to brewing coffee, and we think it makes it taste so much better."

A wave of heat moved across Maggie's face as he looked her way and asked, "So, what's your secret?"

In a snippy tone, she replied, "You know exactly what it is, so don't act like you don't."

Curling the lines in her forehead, Lizzie asked, "Did we miss something?"

Passing the pan of cherry bars, Maggie said, "It's nothing other than Henry was the one who told me to add a pinch of salt to the coffee grounds to cut the bitterness."

Teena took a sip of her coffee before saying, "Aren't you full of surprises?" Placing her cup on the table and looking in Henry's direction, she asked, "So, what else can we learn about Henry Schrock from Indiana?"

Maggie didn't let him answer before she said, "I think he has better things to do than let the two of you hammer him with questions all afternoon."

Clearing his throat, Henry piped in. "Let me have it. What else do you want to know?"

Lizzie took it as an invitation and added, "So did all of your *bruders* and *schwesters* settle in Indiana?"

Maggie noticed a flash of concern cover his face as he answered in a solemn tone. "All but one. My older *schwester* and her family still run the coffee shop, and all ten of my *bruders* work in one form or another at Schrock Construction.

Sensing the change in his tone, Maggie took it upon herself to change the subject. "Henry needs your help."

Lizzie took a napkin from the center of the table, and wiped her mouth before saying, "We're all ears, shoot."

Henry looked in Maggie's direction and asked, "Do you have paper and something I can write with?"

Without responding, Maggie went to the drawer and retrieved a yellow pad and pencil and handed it to him before she sat back down.

Taking a few seconds to write something across the top of the tablet, he asked, "How much do you know about Mrs. Sorensen and the farm across the street from the Inn?"

Teena leaned back in her chair and said, "Maybe more than most, I suppose."

Lizzie picked up a spoon and added sugar to her cup and said. "We've been around long enough to know she had a fond spot for that farm and was in no hurry to sell it. It's sat empty for years."

Teena was quick to add. "When Noah Beiler died, she bought it up quick."

"I think his oldest works at the Inn, Amanda. I think her name is?" Teena added.

"She works in the kitchen," Maggie replied.

Running his hand through his hair and pushing it off to the side, Henry asked, "If she had a soft spot for it, why on earth would she agree to let someone come in with plans to bulldoze it? There's plenty of commercial properties closer to the Outlet Mall that would be better suited; it doesn't make sense."

Maggie tapped her fingers on the table and said, "There has to be more to the story. I wonder how much Amanda knows about the Inn and Mrs. Sorensen? She might be able to fill in some missing pieces."

"What I don't understand is why a company from New York would have an interest in a little town like Willow Springs?"

Lizzie and Teena both look at each other and in unison said, "Marcellus shale."

"Shale?" Maggie asked.

Clicking her tongue and shaking her head from side to side, Lizzie answered, "It wouldn't be the first time a big company tried to come in and talk landowners into signing a lease to drill for natural gas. I suspect since the Beiler farm is about three hundred acres, it would make it a prime location."

"Do you think Mrs. Sorensen knows about the shale?" Maggie asked.

Teena spoke up. "I can't see how she wouldn't know about it. It was in all the papers a few years back about the line of shale that runs through Willow Springs. The Bishop met with all the Amish landowners throughout the county, and they unanimously agreed not to sell or lease any land to any company interested in drilling for gas."

Leaning back in his chair and folding his arms across his chest, he said, "Things are starting to make sense. I bet they're using the bakery as a diversion."

"What do you mean a diversion?" Maggie asked.

"According to the plat map, the property is long and narrow, and it'd be easy to build an access road at the back of the property. I bet they're counting on making the bakery a tourist attraction to keep attention off what they really want the property for. I've seen it happen before. Companies come in making big promises to add tourist dollars to the local economy, and once they do, people turn a blind eye to shady business deals."

Worry lines etched in Lizzie's forehead as she asked, "Tourist attraction? What on earth does he have planned?"

Chapter 12

Cinnamon Waffles

Maggie woke up early, anxious to get to the Inn on her first day without Mrs. Sorensen. Pulling the blue pleated curtain away from her bedroom window, she used her hand to melt the frost and peered outside. The snow had blown up on the windowpane, and the wind whistled around the house. Not taking time for so much as a cup of tea, she left a note and pulled her wool coat and bonnet tightly around her before moving outside.

Quietly shutting the door, she stood on the front porch for a few moments before stepping off in the snow. The quietness of the early morning hour gave way to the booming sounds of a snowplow as it passed. At least ten inches of new snow had covered the ground, and its light and fluffy texture made it easy to maneuver through. Silently thanking the Lord that it was not wet and heavy, she wasted no time in following the freshly made tracks in the road.

As she rounded the bend closest to the Inn, the lights from the porch guided her way. Looking much like a picture postcard blanketed in fresh snow, she smiled at its beauty. The farm across the street only added to its charm. Stopping for a minute at the fence, a sense of longing for the empty house captivated her. With a gloved hand, she tenderly brushed snow from the top rail and understood Henry's pull to the abandoned farm. It was such a shame it sat cold and empty and didn't have a family warming its rooms.

The morning light was starting to make the horizon bright as she walked around to the back of the Inn. The snow had blown a small drift up against the back door. Reaching for the shovel, she pushed piles of snow away from the door and cleared the sidewalk. Stopping to take a breath, she leaned on the shovel and looked across the street. The morning sky added color behind the old farmhouse, and for a split-second, she saw herself standing on its porch. Closing her eyes, she let the comforting image form in her mind. Shaking her head and pushing the silly notions away, she positioned the shovel up against the white clapboard house and stomped the snow from her boots before entering.

The warmth of the Inn and the essential oils strategically placed through the Inn gave the home its familiar scent as she made her way to the kitchen. Opening the door, she found Henry and Bella sitting at the small table in the corner of the room.

"Bella, you're here."

Bella stood and walked to the sink to dispose of her cup before she answered, "I was afraid of the storm and didn't want to be late, so I had my roommate drive me over last night. I stayed in Henry's room. I hope that was okay?"

No words escaped Maggie's lips as she tried to comprehend what the girl had said. The thoughts swirling around in her head must have turned her face a shade of gray because Henry was quick to add.

"I slept on the floor and gave her my bed."

Bella picked up a towel and wiped the counter as she said, "I hope you don't mind. I started coffee as soon as I got up, and Henry started a fire in the sitting room."

Trying to sound appreciative of the effort the girl was putting forth, Maggie nodded her head in approval and said, "Thank you."

Hearing the chime of the back door as it opened, Maggie said. "That must be Amanda."

Henry was quick to add. "I'll leave you ladies to your work." Looking toward Bella, he said in a loving tone. "We'll talk more later."

Maggie watched as Bella looked in his direction and nodded her head in agreement. She couldn't help but notice the tender way she looked at him, even though it left a twisted knot in her stomach.

~~

Standing at the desk in the foyer, Maggie read through her notes, trying to follow the step-by-step directions. Pushing the delete button to clear all the phone messages, she looked at the list of cancellations wishing there were an easier way to update them than using the computer.

She was staring at the blank screen when Bella walked up beside her.

"I was intimidated by it at first too," Bella said as she reached around her and held the power button down until the blue screen appeared. Waiting until a mountain scene had loaded, she asked, "What is the password?"

Maggie looked at her notes and read. "AppleBlossom1902"

Bella stood back, pointed to the keyboard, and said. "Go ahead and type it in."

With one finger, Maggie typed it in the box and hit the enter key. When the screen popped up about a wrong password, she looked to Bella for help.

Looking over at the notes, Bella asked, "Did you use a capital B and A?"

Without answering, she tried again.

Picking back up the cleaning bucket, Bella started to walk away as she said, "You should be good to go."

In a pleading voice, Maggie said, "Please don't go. I don't want to do anything wrong; you know more about computers than I do."

Bella sat her bucket back down and came to stand closer.

Maggie followed her instructions one line at a time as she maneuvered the booking program. It only took a few minutes to cancel the reservations and check on any new ones before she closed the program and breathed a sigh of relief.

"Whew, I guess it wasn't as hard as I was making it. Thanks for sticking around."

"No problem. I remember when I first started using one for school, I thought I'd never get the hang of it. Thank goodness my roommate had a lot of patience."

There was something so sweet about Bella that Maggie couldn't help but like. Regardless of her growing feelings for Henry, she knew why he was drawn to her. Picking up the clipboard and heading to the kitchen, she looked over at Bella and asked, "Why did you leave?"

There was an understanding between them that didn't need an explanation. Bella's accent couldn't hide the fact she was raised Amish regardless of if she wore English clothes.

Following her through the kitchen door and taking time to answer, Bella put her bucket in the supply closet and said, "I wanted more than what Elkhart could offer. I came to Willow Springs with friends and stayed long after they went home. I found a job at the Outlet Mall, learned to drive, and took my GED."

Bella sat on a stool at the island and reached for a mug to pour herself a cup of coffee before continuing. "It took a couple of years, but

I saved enough to take a few college classes. Not sure if I'll ever finish, but for right now, it's what I do."

Holding the mug in both hands and blowing the hot liquid, she said in a playful tone. "If Henry had his way, he'd pack me up and send me back to Indiana on the next bus."

Maggie leaned back on the counter by the sink and said, "I can tell he cares for you."

"I'm sure he does, and I know he means well. But I'm not ready to go home yet." Pausing long enough to take a sip from her mug, she changed the subject and asked, "So why did you leave? Henry mentioned you're from Wisconsin."

"Well, it's a long story, but let's just say I didn't leave on my own accord. But unlike you, I'd like nothing more than to hop on the next bus heading west."

Turning her attention to Amanda, who had quietly been observing their conversation, Maggie asked, "Since we're getting to know one another, have you always lived in Willow Springs?"

Softly she answered, "Was born and raised right across the street."

In a questioning tone, Maggie asked, "What happened?"

"My *datt* was killed in a farming accident a few years back, and with a family of eight girls, we couldn't take care of it. *Mamm* sold it to Mrs. Sorensen, and we moved to a smaller house down the road."

Taking a few seconds to read the recipe in front of her, Amanda poured milk into a measuring cup and continued in a sorrowful voice. "It breaks my heart every time I walk past our house. It's a shame it sits empty, and now Mr. Waldorf is going to tear it down. I haven't told my *mamm* yet. It will kill her when she hears about it."

Taking a whisk from the stone crock in the middle of the island, Amanda beat eggs into the milk as she said, "Mrs. Sorensen bought our farm to help *Mamm*. But I never understood why she did; she had no intention of using it."

Moving to stand next to Amanda, Maggie asked, "What else do you know about Mrs. Sorensen?"

"Not too much. *Mamm* used to take care of her daughter when she was sick, and after she died, she changed. *Mamm* always says, when a child dies, a part of a mother dies too. I guess that's what happened."

Maggie leaned on the island and said, "I suppose that explains a lot."

"She wasn't always like that," Amanda said.

"What about Mr. Waldorf?" Maggie asked.

"He and his wife have been coming here for years. That's all I know."

Amanda slowly stirred the milk mixture into the bowl of flour and sugar and continued. "I haven't worked here too long, but I don't trust him. There's something about him that makes Mrs. Sorensen edgy when he's here."

Maggie leaned in toward both girls and, in a hushed tone, said. "Let's keep our eyes and ears open. If we can figure out what pull Mr. Waldorf has on Mrs. Sorensen, maybe we can help Henry save Willow Springs."

Picking up the recipe card from the counter and looking at the ingredients in front of them, Maggie asked, "There's no baking powder here. Did you remember to put it in?"

"Oh my. No, I didn't. Thanks for catching that. See what I mean? I don't have the knack for cooking."

Maggie smiled and patted the girl on the shoulder. "We make a great team."

Bella warmed up her coffee. "Where is Mrs. Sorensen today?"

Maggie picked up her clipboard and answered, "All she said is she needed to go to Pittsburgh for a few days. It must have been pretty important to leave us here by ourselves. She was certain we could handle things while she was gone, but I'm not too sure. What are we going to do about all of these cancellations?"

"Do you know if she has any social media accounts?" Bella asked. "We could put a post up that we have rooms for anyone traveling through the area. That might bring some people off the Interstate."

Maggie looked over at Amanda. "Have you ever heard her mention anything?"

"Not to me," Amanda said as she added a teaspoon of baking powder to the batter.

Turning her attention back to Bella, Maggie said, "What a great idea, but I wouldn't know the first thing about doing that."

“I still have a list of things to do; I'll check into it when I’m done. Maybe we can fill the rooms back up with people trying to escape the storm.” Before carrying her cup to the sink, Bella brushed sugar crumbs off the counter and into her cup and said, "If I didn't know better, you'd think I was the one cooking in here. I make such a mess too."

Amanda's face turned a slight shade of pink and giggled before saying, "A messy kitchen makes for happy tummies my *mamm* always says."

Stirring the batter and lifting the full whisk over the bowl, Amanda frowned as the lumpy batter dropped into the glass container. "I can't say there will be many happy tummies with these waffles."

In a questioning tone, Maggie asked, "Waffles? The batter is way too thick for that."

"I was trying to make these cinnamon waffles, but I must have done something wrong."

Picking up the recipe card and reading over the ingredients, Maggie asked, "Did you melt the butter first?"

Dropping the whisk in the bowl, forcing a glob of batter to splash on the floor, Amanda said in a huff. "See what I mean, the kitchen's no place for me."

Trying to lighten the mood, Bella wrapped her arm around Amanda's shoulder and said, "I feel the same way about cleaning. I don't enjoy it in the least."

Maggie laid the recipe card down, put her hands on her hips, and said in a reassuring tone. "I have an idea. Amanda, you take over Bella's cleaning chores, Bella work on drumming up some reservations, and I'll take care of getting breakfast ready."

"Really?" Amanda asked in a hopeful tone.

Maggie dumped the batter in the trash and replied, "Why not? We only have three guests, and Mrs. Sorensen isn't here. I see no harm in it."

"I think it's a great idea," Bella said as she handed Amanda her cleaning list and headed to the door. "I'll start by checking if the Inn has any social media accounts."

Amanda didn't move and waited until Bella had left the room before she asked, "Are you sure we won't get in trouble for this. You know what a short fuse Mrs. Sorensen has."

Maggie patted her arm and said in a reassuring tone, "She left me in charge, didn't she? Now go, let me handle breakfast, and you get the rooms ready. Hopefully, Bella can stir up some reservations, and we'll have a full Inn for when she gets back."

~~

Drizzling brown sugar and butter over the hot waffles and adding a spoon of sweetened cream cheese over the top, Maggie smiled at the outcome. Pushing the door open with her hip, she carried two plates to the dining room. Mr. and Mrs. Waldorf had already found their seats at the table, and Henry was just walking into the room.

"What do we have here?" Mrs. Waldorf asked. "Whatever it is, it smells heavenly."

"Cinnamon waffles with cream cheese icing," Maggie answered as she placed the plates in front of them.

Without looking in Henry's direction, she said, "I'll be right back with yours."

Alone in the kitchen, she added an extra spoon of icing to Henry's waffles and carried it to the dining room. Placing the plate in front of him, she stopped for only a brief second to top his coffee off and ask if he needed anything else.

Without looking up, he said, "I'm good, thank you."

Taking that as her clue to leave, she couldn't help but be disappointed that he hadn't so much as looked at her: no winks, no smiles, no charming conversation.

Chapter 13

Cinnamon Rolls

Pulling his collar around the back of his neck, Henry stood on the porch, watching winter lay a new layer of snow across the countryside. The farm across the street held his attention as he let the fresh air clear his mind.

It was becoming tiresome talking to Mr. Waldorf about moving his project closer to the Interstate. The older man was trying his patience and had no interest in giving up the hold he had on the three hundred acres. There was no reasoning with him, and when he excused himself to take a phone call, Henry stepped outside.

Hearing the scrape of a shovel on the sidewalk, he looked over to the side of the porch as Maggie pushed snow from the walkway. Without hesitating, he moved in her direction and took the shovel from her hands.

"You don't need to do that; I'm more than capable of shoveling snow," she said as she reluctantly released the handle.

"I'm sure you are, but right now, I could use some manual labor."

"How's it going in there? Are you making any headway in figuring out what's going on?"

In a gruff tone, he answered, "There's no reasoning with him, and all I've been able to figure out is he has investors he has to answer too."

Adding the last scoop of snow to the pile at the corner of the house, he leaned on the shovel and said, "This project is bigger than just him. His investors want to meet with me this afternoon. He's in there right now setting up a phone conference. If I can find out who they are, maybe I'll be able to figure out if they have any holdings in the mining industry."

Handing her back the shovel, he turned toward the steps and said, "I best get back in there."

Leaning the shovel up against the corner by the back door, she stomped her boots off before going inside. No sooner had she hung up her coat than Bella called her name.

"Maggie, where are you?"

"I'm back here, what's the matter?"

Walking to meet her in the hallway, Bella said, "Nothing other than the post I made on social media is working. We got a call from a young couple traveling north to Buffalo. They're anxious to find a room."

Grabbing her hand and leading her to the sitting room where the television was on, she said, "The local news posted a Winter Weather Advisory for Northwestern Pennsylvania and Northeastern Ohio. They're talking about shutting Interstate 79 and 80 down."

Before she even had a chance to respond, the phone rang, and Bella left to answer it.

Standing in the doorway, Maggie listened as the weatherman pointed to the map indicating all areas affected by the storm. With her attention directed at the black box on the wall, she failed to notice Mrs. Waldorf sitting in the chair near the fireplace.

Laying her needlepoint down and taking a sip of her tea, the small woman said in a hushed tone. "I haven't seen a storm like this in years. I'm sure glad we decided to stay a few days longer. Had George and Henry finished their business yesterday as they planned, we would have been on the road driving in this. The good Lord knew what he was doing."

Not taking her eyes off the television, Maggie said in a caring nature. "You certainly will be more comfortable here. We have plenty of firewood to keep you warm, and we have your favorite tea."

Picking back up her needlepoint, she glanced Maggie's way and said. "I couldn't ask for anything more, and I'm glad to ride out the storm right here in this chair, snuggled up to the warm fire."

Walking back in the room, Bella stopped and looked Maggie's way. "The hotel near the Mall is on the phone. They have a group of twelve women who are trying to make it back to Pittsburgh looking for rooms. They rented out their last one and were hoping they could send them this way."

"Oh my, twelve! We only have seven available rooms." Maggie exclaimed in a concerned voice.

"I told the Hotel Manager that, and he said a few of the women agreed to share a room."

"Then, I say send them our way."

Bella turned to relay the message as Maggie went to the kitchen. She already sent Amanda home, with instructions to deliver a message to her aunts.

Opening the pantry, she took an inventory of the supplies and then headed to the freezer. Typically, they only served breakfast, but if the snowstorm lasted for any length of time, she'd need to feed twenty people. Taking a deep breath, she started to outline a few meal ideas on the pad in front of her.

Bella bolted through the swinging door and said, "They should be here in less than twenty minutes. Is there anything I can do?"

In a nervous giggle, Maggie said, "Your guess is as good as mine. I think we're going to have to wing it. Amanda cleaned all the rooms before she left, and I just checked on food. We should be good for a few days. I told Amanda to tell my aunts I'd be staying if the weather got too bad."

Bella pulled a stool out at the island and said, "My classes got canceled for the rest of the week, so I'm all yours."

Tapping the pencil on the counter, Maggie tried to figure out how to bring up the subject of her staying in Henry's room. "I certainly need your help, but only if you find other sleeping arrangements."

Raising her eyebrow, Bella looked at her in confusion and said. "I'm sure he doesn't mind, but if you're uncomfortable, I'll find somewhere else to sleep."

Bothered that she didn't see anything wrong with the situation, Maggie answered in a sharp tone. "Mrs. Sorensen has two sofas in her office; we can use those."

The chime of the front door replaced the awkward silence at the same time as Henry peered his head around the kitchen door.

"Am I interrupting anything?" Henry asked as he looked her way.

"No, not at all. What do you need?"

"A quiet place where we can take a conference call."

Bella slipped around Henry, as she said. "I bet that's our couple now. I'll go take care of them."

Maggie followed Bella to the door as she answered Henry. "Let's move you into Mrs. Sorensen's office. That way, you can shut the door and won't be bothered."

"Let me go gather our things and tell Mr. Waldorf we're moving out of the dining room," he said.

Taking the key from her pocket, Maggie headed to the office. Once inside, she cleared Mrs. Sorensen's desk and neatly stacked the folders on the stand near the window. Patting the sides of the folders making sure they were in a stable pile, her eye caught the name written on the yellow tab. "*Waldorf Company.*"

Her curiosity was disturbed when Mr. Waldorf came through the door loudly, asking, "Does the phone have a speaker? And can we do a three-way call?"

Maggie walked to the phone and looked over its buttons and said, "I have no idea."

Laying his briefcase on the desk and moving the tube of blueprints from his arm to the chair, he said, "Get out of my way, so I can figure it out." As she backed up, he mumbled, "Why my wife likes to stay here is beyond me."

Looking toward Henry, she said, "We're expecting a houseful so you can use the office as long as you need."

Stopping what he was doing, Mr. Waldorf barked, "A houseful! We stay here because it's quiet, how do you expect me to get any work done? When will Mrs. Sorensen be back?"

Standing up straight and facing Mr. Waldorf, Maggie replied, "I can assure you we'll be able to handle the extra guests, and you won't be bothered back here. As far as Mrs. Sorensen, she didn't say, but I'm sure it won't be today with the storm."

Walking to the door and pausing, she asked, "Is there anything else I can do for you?"

Pulling the phone closer and sitting in the leather chair behind the desk, Mr. Waldorf grumbled something inaudible and dismissed her with the back of his hand.

Leaning in as she passed, Henry whispered, "Thank you."

Walking toward the front of the Inn, Maggie marveled as Bella gracefully checked the young couple in and directed them to their room at the top of the stairs.

Waiting until the new guests left the foyer, Maggie said, "Thank you for taking care of them. Not sure what I would've done without you today." Pushing a loose strand of hair under her *kapp*, she added, "I wish I hadn't sent Amanda home."

Looking down the hallway, Bella asked, "What is Mr. Waldorf all in a huff about? He stormed out of the dining room like the place was on fire."

"All I know is he wants quiet, and I'm not sure he'll get that with twelve women showing up any minute."

Bella clicked her fingers over the keyboard of the laptop with ease as she completed the check-in and said, "Henry can handle him. It won't be the first time he's had to deal with a difficult client, and I'm sure it won't be the last."

The familiarity Bella had with him left Maggie wanting to understand their connection, but without giving it another thought, the door chime rang, and the foyer filled with a houseful of cheerful voices.

~~

Every corner of the Inn was filled, and Bella and Maggie did their best to make everyone comfortable. Just as Maggie took a tray of cinnamon rolls from the oven, Bella came through the door handing her the phone whispering, "Mrs. Sorensen."

Setting the hot tray down, she wiped her hands on her pink apron and took the phone. Her stomach flipped as she prepared herself for Mrs. Sorensen's wrath.

"Mrs. Sorensen. How are you?"

In a harsh tone, she asked, "Margaret, why is Bella answering the phone? That's your job."

"Yes ma'am, I know, but she's been a great help. Every room is full."

"What do you mean full?

"The hotel at the Interstate called and asked if we had any rooms, and Bella put something out on social media."

"She did what? Who gave her permission to do that?"

"I guess I did."

"We'll deal with that later. I only called to tell you the storm has the highways closed, and I won't be able to get out of Pittsburgh for a couple of days."

"I think we have everything under control."

"You'll need to stay at the Inn until I return."

"I planned on it. I figured I'd sleep on the sofa in your office."

"There is no need to do that. You have my room key, use that."

"Okay, thank you. One thing, Mr. Waldorf needed a place to take a conference call, so I let him use your office."

Raising her voice, Mrs. Sorensen said, "You did what? There's a folder on my desk he can't see."

"I moved everything off your desk to the stand near the window."

"Margaret, listen to me. You march right in that office and take everything you took from my desk and move it to my room. Do you understand?"

Pausing for a moment, Maggie asked, "Right now? They have the door closed, and I'll be interrupting them."

"Yes, now."

Without so much of a goodbye, Mrs. Sorensen ended the call leaving Maggie with a sense of uneasiness.

Handing the phone back to Bella, she said, "She wants me to move some papers out of her office."

"Now?"

"Yes, now. Mr. Waldorf isn't going to be happy. Wish me luck."

Taking in a deep breath, Maggie willed herself to turn the knob. As she opened the door, both Henry and Mr. Waldorf looked her way.

Pointing to the stack of folders on the stand, she mouthed, "I need those."

Mr. Waldorf glared her way without missing a beat in the heated conversation he was having with the man on the other end of the phone.

As she gathered the papers, she couldn't help but overhear the man ask Henry a question. A warm assurance filled her as he answered in a calm but authoritative manner.

"Schrock Construction will have no part of this project if it means Amish businesses may suffer. You have to understand these cottage businesses may be their only form of income."

In a stern but professional voice, the man on the phone said, "Mr. Schrock, you have to understand this is business. As soon as Mrs. Sorensen signs the final papers, we will be building Waldorf Bakery and an Amish Home Goods Store on that property. Regardless, if you handle the project or not, we will be moving forward."

Maggie carried the stack of folders to the door and slipped out as quietly as she entered. Softly pushing the door shut, she waited, hoping to hear Henry respond. Leaning her ear up to the crack in the door, she heard him say.

"I find it hard to believe the Lawrence County Planning Commission will approve this project."

Recognizing the curt voice of Mr. Waldorf, he said, "You have to understand the county will be more interested in the economic impact the tourist dollars will have than worrying about upsetting a few Amish farmers."

Henry was quick to ask. "But why Willow Springs? The commercial property closer to Grove City is better suited for a project like this."

The voice on the phone said, "As I've explained before, we're not interested in any other property.

Maggie couldn't listen to one more word. A sense of defeat filled her as she carried the folders to Mrs. Sorensen's room. Laying the stack on the dresser, the pull to know what was inside left her in an intrigued state. Leaving the unanswered questions behind, she locked the door and headed to the kitchen.

Chapter 14

Buttermilk Biscuits

Maggie stood at the sink, washing the last of the pans she'd used to make chicken noodle soup. Her buttermilk biscuits had been a hit, and she smiled as she remembered Henry savoring their buttery texture. The Inn had finally settled down, and most of the guests had retired to their rooms. A few of them stayed to watch the ten o'clock news, and Maggie heard their muffled voices echo off the Inn's twelve-foot ceilings.

The last time she checked, Henry was in deep conversation with the young couple who had checked in earlier that afternoon. Bella had tidied up the dining room and headed to bed. Earlier, she left blankets and a pillow on the sofa in Mrs. Sorensen's office for her to use.

Drying her hands on a towel, Maggie leaned over the sink, checking to see if the snow had let up. The light on the corner of the Inn did little to illuminate the courtyard, as snow dulled its brightness. Remembering she needed to fill the wood box near the fireplace, she untied her apron and hung it on the peg in the supply closet and headed to the back door. Sitting on the bench, she pulled on her boots and bundled up tight to venture outdoors. Before opening the door, she listened as the wind whistled around the Inn, and she braced herself for its bitterness.

The snow had blown up against the back door, and it took an extra push to get it opened enough she could slip outside. Taking a few minutes to shovel it away, she waited until her eyes adjusted to the darkness before heading to the woodshed. The path to the tin covered building was knee-deep with snow, and it made its way over the top of her boots and caked itself on her black stockings. The wind made a swooshing sound as it caught up under her skirt and took her breath away with its brutal chill.

Sliding the door open, she entered the building and pushed the door closed. Reaching in her pocket for the flashlight, she turned it on and scanned the building looking for the cloth wood tote used to carry wood inside. Locating it hanging on a hook, she reached for it without realizing she had shut her skirt in the door. Turning to pull it free, she lost her balance and fell into the neatly stacked cord of wood. In a split-second, the flashlight flew from her hands, and she found herself at the bottom of a woodpile. Laying on the cold dirt floor, it took her a minute to realize what happened. In an instant, a sharp pain filled her thigh as she tried to reach the light that was just out of arms reach.

For the next few minutes, she worked tirelessly to move the wood from her legs, but a sticky warmth trickled down her leg, leaving her dizzy. Closing her eyes and laying her head back on the earthen floor, she heard her name in the distance before darkness overcame her.

~~

Henry flipped the lights off in the sitting room and made his way to the kitchen to check on Bella and Maggie. Pushing the kitchen door open, he was surprised it was empty. Noticing Maggie's apron hanging on the back of the closet door, he flipped off the light, assuming they'd gone to bed. On the way to the stairs, he fought off a sense of anxiousness. Confident it was remnants of his meeting with Mr. Waldorf, he pushed the man from his thoughts and let visions of Maggie's wheat-colored hair fill his head.

Quietly making his way up the stairs, he smiled as thoughts of how she graciously tended to each guest, warmed his heart. With unsettling thoughts of Maggie and the persistent way Bella told him she wasn't moving back to Indiana, he stood at the window overlooking the courtyard below. The wind was blowing small circles around the light that left shadows on the ground below. Catching movement and a flash of light, he rubbed his palm on the window to get a clearer view. Light bounced off the dark fabric as it blew in the wind, telling him it could only be Maggie.

Taking his coat and hat off the hook by the door, he struggled to put them on as he ran down the steps. In a frustrated state, he thought. *What is she thinking, going outside at this hour?* Without even buttoning his coat, he ran outside, calling her name in the dark.

Following her footsteps, he looked toward the building in front of him. Stopping to slide the door on its track, he struggled as if something on the other side was preventing it from opening. When she didn't answer, an unexpected bout of adrenaline took over as he pulled the door off its track. When he saw no movement in the dark building, he stepped off to the side, hoping the light on the corner of the house would fill the space.

Catching sight of the dim light on the floor, he stooped to retrieve the flashlight. Scanning the room, he stopped when Maggie's white *kapp* strings caught the light. Her outer bonnet lay crooked on her head, and the white satin ribbons glowed brightly against the beam of light. Dropping to his knees, he leaned in closer to feel her breath on his cheek. Shining the light toward her feet, he quickly went to work removing the pile of wood that had engulfed her.

Starting at her calf and working his way up her body, he gently felt for any apparent signs of injury. When his hand made it to her thigh, moisture-filled his palm. Positioning the light on her leg, he softly pushed the blue material up, revealing a deep gash. Without thinking twice, he tore a strip of fabric from the bottom of her dress and tied it around her leg to stop the bleeding. Once he was confident, she had no other injuries, he scooped her up and held her tight in his arms. As snow fell on her face, she instinctively tucked her head in the crook of his neck, returning from her brief unconsciousness.

Letting out a small moan, Henry reassured her by shielding her face with his own, blocking the wind as he whispered in her ear. "It's okay. I've got you. Let me get you to the house, and we can see about your leg."

Reaching to open the door with the hand he had under her legs, he pushed the door open so hard it bounced off the wall, making an alarming sound. Hollering for Bella as he passed the office door, he stopped at Mrs. Sorensen's private quarters and sighed when the door wouldn't open.

Alarmed by the sudden noise, Bella barreled out of the office as Henry stopped at the locked door.

"Oh my, what happened?" She asked.

"Unlock this door." He demanded.

"I don't have the key; she keeps it in her apron pocket."

Henry motioned his head to the kitchen and said, "Her apron is hanging on the door in there."

Bella retrieved the key and unlocked the room. Henry gently laid her on the bed and shook the feeling back in his arms and said, "She's cut her leg on something. She must have caught it on a nail or a piece of metal when she fell in the woodshed."

"The woodshed? What on earth were you doing out there at this time of the night?" Bella asked as she pushed her dress up over her knee.

Not giving Maggie time to answer, Henry added, "Bringing wood in. I saw her from my bedroom window and followed her."

Moving closer to the top of the bed, he said, "Good thing I did, you could have frozen to death out there."

Maggie tried to sit up and said, "I wanted to make sure the wood box was full."

Standing back and turning his head as Bella revealed Maggie's bare leg, he said, "All you had to do was ask. I would have taken care of it."

Flinching when Bella removed the makeshift tourniquet, she gasped when she saw the gash on the side of her thigh and said through gritted teeth. "You're a guest. It's not your responsibility to fill the wood box."

Covering the wound back up with the cloth Henry had torn from her skirt, Bella asked, "Do you have any idea if we have an emergency kit?"

Before Maggie had a chance to answer, Henry piped in. "I have one better than that. The young man, Mr. Trenton, who checked in this afternoon, is an EMT. I'll get him."

Taking the stairs two at a time, he stopped at the couple's room and softly knocked on the door.

Watching it open, just enough so the slender dark-haired man could see out, he asked in a sleepy voice. "What is it?"

"I'm sorry to bother you, but Maggie's cut her leg, and I'm hoping you could take a look at it."

Without any hesitation, the man reached for his keys off the table by the door and said, "I have a First-Aid kit in my trunk. Go get it, and I'll get dressed."

~~

Bella pushed Henry out of Maggie's room as Mr. Trenton tended to the wound. Henry's rush of adrenaline subsided with a need for something to calm his nerves. Giving no thought to the late hour, he opened the pantry looking for a quick instant fix. He located the black crystals and headed to the stove to heat water. Sitting on a stool in the center of the room, he ran his hand through his hair, which he found himself doing a lot lately. No matter how hard he tried to deny it, Maggie Fisher had gotten under his skin. The problem was, she made it clear she had no interest in him more than figuring out how to stop Mr. Waldorf from monopolizing the community.

The whistle from the teapot diverted his attention momentarily as he tried to pinpoint what changed since their walk into town. There was no sense in denying it; there was something about the girl that drew him in. It was like a magnet from the very first time he spotted her on the bus. He certainly was not having much luck talking Bella into going back to Elkhart. Maybe he'd stay in Willow Springs to see if there was anything hopeful behind Maggie's hazel-green eyes.

Carrying his cup of instant coffee to the front room, he stood in the darkened room and looked out over the farmland across the street. Not that he could see anything further than the porch railing, he played a variety of scenarios over in his head. What could Mrs. Sorensen have to gain by holding on to the property so long? If she knew about the shale that ran through Willow Springs, was she holding out for the highest bidder? He couldn't believe she would agree to build something like the Amish Home Goods Store so close to the Inn. Surely, she knew it would affect the lively hood of so many of her neighbors. None of it made sense. But more importantly, the uneasiness he had about Mr. Waldorf and his investors weighed heavily on his mind. He was sure they would do nothing short of paying off the planning commission to get their project approved.

Chapter 15

Overnight Apple Sticky Buns

Lizzie stood at the stove, adding small pieces of kindling to the firebox as Teena filled the white porcelain tea kettle with water. The early morning light was having trouble making it's way up over the horizon as snow left Willow Springs blanketed in a gray haze.

"I wonder how Maggie's making out?" Teena asked as she placed the kettle on the cast iron stovetop.

Lizzie pulled a chair out at the table and said. "Hopefully, she's been able to spend a good bit of time getting to know Henry. If not, we need to put a plan in place."

"What do you have in mind?"

Teena pulled two mugs from the cupboard and said. "Isn't it funny how they both landed in Willow Springs at the same time? It's like the good Lord already had a plan. Maybe he doesn't need our help this time."

Lizzie added a tea bag to her cup, as she said, "All I know is Henry hung on her every word, and she got all tongue-tied around him. Sometimes these young folks need a push in the right direction."

Glancing out the window over the sink, Teena said, "This snow may work in our favor. No chance of him leaving within the next few days for certain."

Just as the teakettle started to whistle, a loud knock startled them, and Teena headed to the front door, saying, "Well, I'll be. Who on earth could that be so early?"

A blast of winter swirled in as Teena opened the door as a snow-covered Henry stood on the front stoop.

"Henry, my goodness, what are you doing out in this weather? Come in out of the cold."

Stomping his boots off before entering, he stayed planted on the blue and black braided rug near the door and explained, "Maggie fell and cut her leg last night."

"Oh, my! How bad is it?"

Taking his hat off, he said, "It's a deep gash. Thank goodness one of the guests is an EMT and was able to bandage it up. He said she might need a few stitches, but more importantly, she needs a tetanus shot first thing this morning. We're pretty sure she got caught on a nail."

Standing beside Teena, Lizzie asked, "A nail?"

"She went outside to bring wood in," he answered.

In a concerned tone, Lizzie said, "Not sure how we're going to do that? We won't even be able to get in the barn until one of the neighbors comes to push the snow away."

"That's why I'm here. I'm hoping you'd get a bag together for her and let me borrow the buggy. The snowplows are keeping up with the roads, so I should be able to make it to the clinic."

"Certainly. Will she be coming home?" Teena asked.

"I'm not sure; I guess that'll be up to her. Let me work on clearing the barn door, and I'll be back in for her bag."

Teena closed the door behind him and said in an assuring voice. "I'd say God has this one, don't you think?"

Lizzie made a click with her tongue before responding, "I wouldn't count your chickens before they hatch *schwester*. Maggie's as hard-headed as the rest of the women in this family. I'm sure it's going to take more than a ride to get her to notice Henry Schrock."

~~

Without opening her eyes, Maggie pulled the covers over her head, caught somewhere between slumber and a dream. Trying to sort out the images that were still fresh in her mind, she willed herself to replay the scene in her head.

Walking through an apple orchard, she reached for a branch and pulled a white and pink blossom to her nose. The sweetness brought a smile to her face as movement from across the yard caught her attention. Tied to a hitching post in front of a white clapboard house was a brown-topped buggy. A dark-haired man gently rubbed the nose of a lean dark horse as he looked her way. An inviting wave forced her to let go of the branch and step in his direction. A heaviness on her shoulder forced her to stop as she heard a voice whisper. "It's me he loves."

The sound of metal scraping on the driveway outside her window clouded the picture in her mind. The throbbing pain in her thigh brought her back to reality as she opened her eyes. Reaching under the covers to lightly rub the area that caused her discomfort, she pushed herself to a sitting position. Morning light filtered through the sheer curtains as she looked around the room. Her *kapp* lay neatly on the nightstand, and her tattered dress hung over the chair. Barely remembering Bella helping her get ready for bed, she tried to put the previous night's events in order. Going out so late wasn't the smartest idea, but waking in Henry's arms left her breathless. Had she imagined his concern, or was he bothered by her carelessness?

A soft knock on the door cleared her head as she answered, "Come in."

Bella walked in, carrying her tote bag in one hand and a cup of tea in the other. "How are you feeling?" She asked as she set the steaming mug on the nightstand.

"Quite honestly, I'm embarrassed I've caused such a ruckus."

"Don't be silly; it was an accident. Thank God Henry saw you go outside or who knows what would have happened."

Not wanting to approach the subject of Henry with Bella, Maggie was quick to change the subject.

Reaching out to take her bag from Bella's hand, Maggie asked, "How did this get here?"

"Henry walked to your aunts' this morning."

In a concerned voice, Maggie replied, "In this weather? What was he thinking? "

Letting out a small giggle as she turned to shut the door, Bella asked, "Do you need help? Henry has the buggy outside, ready to take you to the clinic."

In an agitated tone, Maggie said, "The clinic? I don't have time to go anywhere. I have breakfast to make, and we have an Inn full of guests. There's no way I'm going anywhere."

Maggie slid to the end of the bed and gently pulled her leg over as Bella helped her slip the cotton nightgown they had found in one of Mrs. Sorensen's drawers over her head.

Taking a clean dark blue dress and fresh stockings from the canvas tote, Bella laid them on the edge of the bed as she said, "Amanda is already here and has breakfast underway. We can manage until you get back."

Pulling the dress over her head, Maggie said in a muffled voice. "I made a double batch of sticky buns last night. They need to set out to raise for another hour or so."

"We're one step ahead of you. Amanda already has them out. So again, we have everything under control. All you need to concern yourself with is getting to the clinic."

With a slight crack in her voice, Maggie said, "Mrs. Sorensen is going to have a fit."

Handing Maggie, the hairbrush she pulled from the bottom of the tote, Bella said, "Well, we don't need to worry about that right now, do we? She's not here, and by the looks of it, there's little chance she'll make it back today."

"Thank goodness," was all Maggie said as she slowly stood and limped her way to the bathroom.

~~

Henry stood at the back door waiting patiently for Maggie. He had already warmed a few bricks in the fireplace, wrapped them in towels, and sat them on the floorboards of the enclosed buggy. Looking out the window, he couldn't help but think the gray skies were an indication; the snow wasn't letting up anytime soon. It wouldn't take but an hour or two for the roads to become impassable again.

Watching as Maggie hobbled down the hallway, he took her coat from the hook and held it open for her. With a look of irritation on her face, she said, "I'm perfectly capable of putting on my own coat."

Not letting her take it from his hands, he said, "I'm sure you are, but right now, I'm helping you with it, so get over it."

In a huff, she put her arms in the wool sleeves and pulled it around her tightly. Taking the heavy bonnet from the hook beside him, she pulled it over her starched white *kapp* and tied it at her chin. "I guess I'm ready. Let's go."

Opening the door, a gust of wind blew snowflakes as big as pennies in their faces as they headed to the waiting buggy. Noticing a fresh layer of snow had already covered the blanket over the horse, he looked to the sky. Taking her elbow as she maneuvered the slippery sidewalk, he was surprised she didn't flinch at his touch.

Reaching for the brown canvas that covered the door, he unsnapped it and pulled it to the side. Standing at the opening, she shuffled from one foot to the other, trying to figure out how she'd get in. Without giving her an option, he effortlessly cradled her in his arms and lifted her to the waiting seat. With an exasperated look, she turned to face him as if to rebuke his action, but no words escaped her opened lips.

Once she was safely inside, he smiled as he snapped the door covering in place and thought to himself. *I quite like leaving her speechless.*

After shaking the snow from the blanket and securing it behind the seat, he climbed inside. Maggie had already covered her lap with the quilt he laid on the bench and sat with her gloved hands folded neatly on her lap. Without saying a word, he clicked his tongue and snapped the reins, making the horse make a big circle in the driveway and head to the road.

"Are you warm enough?"

"I am."

Concentrating on keeping the unfamiliar horse and buggy on the road, he did little to initiate a conversation. It wasn't hard to tell she was annoyed with him, even though he didn't entirely know why.

~~

The cold did little to ease the ache in her thigh as Maggie kept her eyes on the white landscape in front of them. Her stomach flipped as Henry skillfully guided Aunt Lizzie's horse over the snow-covered roads. She had no idea where the clinic was, or how long it would take to make it there, but she was sure he'd gotten directions from someone. Finding it hard not to be irritated, she sat quietly, letting the familiar clip-clop calm her nerves.

Pushing her feet closer to the bricks, she was grateful he'd been so thoughtful to add them to the cold buggy. Instinctively reaching out to grab his arm as a patch of ice forced the carriage to sway, she was alarmed when he looked at her tenderly and said, "It's okay; I got it."

That was all that was needed to break the silence as he asked. "How's the leg this morning?"

"It's throbbing, but that's to be expected, I suppose."

"I can only imagine. Thank God Mr. Trenton looked at it and said we could wait until morning to see a doctor. If not, I would've called the ambulance."

"Oh, heavens, no! She exclaimed."

Watching as Henry guided the horse to the side of the road, she held her breath as a snowplow passed with so much force, it rocked the buggy, and she slid into him. Biting her bottom lip as a sharp pain penetrated the exact spot where her thigh met his, the closeness forced her to let out a small moan. Quickly, she pushed herself away, leaving ample space between them. Without so much as a hesitation, Henry pulled back out into the road and whispered, "Sorry about that."

Without acknowledging his comment, she clenched her hands as they made their way through the center of town past the Sandwich Shoppe and The Mercantile.

Stopping at the red light on South Main Street, Henry strained to read the snow-covered sign and asked, "That does say Route 208, right?"

Leaning up in her seat to get a better view of the sign, she said, "I think so."

Pulling back on the reins to guide the horse to turn right, he said, "Good, your Aunt said the clinic was up here on the left. Shouldn't be too much further now."

In a panicked tone, Maggie exclaimed, "Oh, no!"

"What is it?" Henry asked in an alarmed voice.

"I didn't bring my purse. I have no way of paying."

"Don't scare me like that." Henry said as he relaxed his shoulders. "I have plenty of money with me, so I'll take care of it."

"I couldn't ask you to do that. You've already done enough."

"And what do you expect me to do? Drive clear back to the Inn and start this trip all over again? I hardly think so."

In a quiet tone, she answered, "I guess not. Thank you."

They both saw the sign to the Willow Springs Clinic and said, "There it is."

Pulling the buggy up to the hitching post, he said, "Sit still, and I'll help you in a minute."

Uncovering her lap with the patchwork handmade quilt, she folded it neatly and placed it on the seat beside her. As she laid her hand on her thigh, the heat alarmed her, as it was noticeable even in the cold.

Waiting as he instructed, she admired him as he took time covering the horse with a blanket and securely tying him to the post. A warm spot filled her heart as he made the horse comfortable.

A flurry blew over his shoulder as he held the heavy canvas to the side to help her out. Lifting her leg with both hands to move it over the door edge, she didn't protest when he lifted her from the seat and gently stood her beside him.

"Lean on me, so you don't slip," he said as he wrapped one arm around her back and held a tight grip under her elbow.

"There is a layer of ice under the snow," she said in a shaky voice.

"I think so too. I've got you, and I won't let you fall."

Waiting for the automatic doors to open, she whispered, "I hope we don't have to wait too long. I hate that we have to be out in this, and I really need to get back to the Inn."

"Would you stop worrying about that place? It'll be fine without you for a couple of hours."

In an agitated tone, she said, "A couple of hours?. I can't be gone that long. I have to make sure Amanda gets breakfast out on time and what if Mrs. Sorensen calls? She's going to be furious."

Making her sit in the first chair they came to, Henry said, "Bella is more than capable of making sure everything is taken care of. Now stay here and let me check you in."

Watching him walk away, she cringed at the way he rolled Bella's name so effortlessly off his lips. Their apparent closeness annoyed her, and in an instant, the words "*It's me he loves*" rang in her ears. Before she even had a chance to push the thought away, he came back, holding his hand out to help her up. "The nurse said she could take you right in."

Reaching for her hand, he bent down, forcing her hand up to the back of his neck as he pulled her up at the waist. For a brief moment, her fingers found the softness of his dark curls, and a jolt of energy trickled down her arm. Setting her down, the scent of wet wool and wood smoke filled her nose and reminded her of the first time she took in his smell.

Taking in a small breath and making a slight sound, she tried to push the closeness away, but Henry held her all the tighter and asked, "Are you okay?"

Fighting to form an audible word, she gave up and shook her head as he guided her to the waiting nurse. Once they made it to the door, the nurse turned to Henry and said, "Mr. Fisher, you can wait for your wife here. I'll come for you after the doctor has had a chance to examine her."

Shifting her weight to the nurse as he released his grip, she looked up at him, waiting for him to correct the apparent confusion. With a wink and a smile, he said, "I'm not going anywhere; I'll be right here when you're through."

Chapter 16

French Toast Casserole

Sitting at the end of the examination table, Maggie waited for the nurse to return with Henry. The two shots the doctor had given her before weaving eighteen stitches into her leg left the area numb. Waiting for the doctor to return with instructions, she pulled her dress back over her knees.

It wasn't hard for her to recognize Henry's voice as he approached the curtained room. Sitting up straight as the doctor pulled the drape open, she was greeted with a warm smile as Henry looked her way.

"How's our patient doing?" Henry asked as he twirled his hat in his hand.

Without saying a word, she turned toward the doctor waiting for him to answer.

"All sewed up and ready to go." Pulling a pad from his pocket and clicking the end of his pen, he said, "I'm a little concerned at the redness and warmth around the wound. I want you to stop at the drugstore and fill this prescription for an antibiotic. She already has a slight fever, and I want to stop any infection before it gets a chance to take hold. Change the dressing twice a day and young lady I want you off your feet for at least forty-eight hours."

In an alarmed voice, she said, "Forty-eight hours? I won't be able to do that, I have to work."

"Not for the next two days, you won't." Slapping Henry on the back as he left the room, he added, "I'm sure this strapping young man can take care of himself for a couple of days."

Again, Henry didn't correct their assumption as he smiled as if he was totally enjoying playing the little charade.

Handing Henry the care bag, the nurse said, "Let me get a wheelchair, and we can at least help her to the door."

Speaking louder than needed, Maggie said, "That won't be necessary. I can walk."

Waving her hand over her shoulder, the nurse said, "Doctor's orders."

After placing his hat back on, Henry wrapped his arm around her waist and lifted her to the floor. Letting the nurse slide the chair behind her, Henry played the role of doting husband. The nurse pushed the chair through the double doors and waited as Henry stopped at the front desk to pay the bill. Clenching her fists, she couldn't wait to get to the privacy of the buggy to give him a piece of her mind.

As they waited for Henry, the nurse leaned over and whispered in her ear.

"You girls work way too hard. You let that strong and strapping man of yours wait on you hand and foot."

Looking over her shoulder to protest the nurses' comment, she said, "But he's..."

Stopping her in mid-sentence, the nurse replied, "But nothing. It's not too often a wife gets to sit back and be waited on, enjoy it while it lasts."

Henry walked up beside them just as she was about to set the nurse straight and asked, "Ready?"

The nurse reached down to set the wheelchair brake at the same time he leaned over to pick her up. Before she had a chance to protest, he said in a smug tone. "Doctors orders."

The nurse giggled behind them as he made his way through the automatic exit. Once outside, the wind blew, and without realizing it, she buried her head in the crook of his neck. In the two minutes it took him to carry her across the parking lot, she enjoyed the warmth of his freshly shaven cheek pressed hard against her forehead. Time stood still as she breathed in his fresh scent, and all thoughts of being upset with him escaped her momentarily.

Without pulling her head away from its protected spot, he kept his cheek locked tight against her head. Turning in closer, he whispered, "I don't want to put you down, but I won't be able to unsnap the door."

Slowly he dropped her to her feet and pulled her close to lean on him as he unfastened the covering. Pushing it off to the side, he effortlessly picked her up and set her gently on the seat. Reaching over to retrieve the blue and yellow quilt, he unfolded it and laid it over her lap. Tucking it securely around her, he reached up and tied her bonnet snugly under her chin. Their eyes stayed joined as she let him care for her as tenderly as no one had ever done before.

Sitting alone in the buggy, the heat from her cheeks warmed her face as her heart beat faster than normal. Shaking her head to clear the thoughts, she whispered to herself. *"There you go again, imagining things. Remember, Bella."*

Fiddling with her gloves and smoothing out the edge of the quilt, she followed him as he made his way around the buggy and up into his seat.

Without saying a word, he turned the horse around and headed for the highway. There was a tautness in the air, much like a secret floating between them, neither one of them brave enough to tell.

A thick layer of white clouded the area in front of the buggy as he struggled to see the road. Keeping the horse to a slow and steady trot, he pulled the reins and guided him into the barren drugstore parking lot. Once he came to a stop, he held his hand out for the folded piece of paper, she held tightly. Softly taking it from her gloved hand, he lingered at her eyes and pulled it from her fingertip without saying a word.

~~

The three miles to the Inn seemed like a hundred as Henry guided the horse one step at a time. His fingers ached as he held onto the reins keeping both horse and buggy within the absent lines of the road. Not familiar with the landscape, he worried that one wrong turn would end them in a snowbank. With an overwhelming need to protect Maggie, he prayed they would make it back safely.

Wishing they didn't need to make another stop, he reluctantly pulled into the drugstore. Reaching for the prescription, he only allowed his eyes to meet hers for a few moments before breaking the magnetic pull she had on him.

Letting the brisk air cool his face, he tucked the paper in his pocket, tied the horse to the post, and ventured inside. Laying the doctor's instructions on the counter, he waited patiently as he looked out the drive-up window. The building at least fifty feet from the drugstore was scarcely visible, forcing his jaw to clench. He should have asked one of the English guests to drive them to the clinic. What was he thinking bringing her out in this weather? The buggy was equipped with turning signals and a headlight; however, the lone orange triangle on the back gave him little comfort in such blinding conditions. Turning from the counter and sitting in one of the chairs off to the side, all he could do was remove his hat and pray. Closing his eyes, he asked God to be with them on their journey.

"Mr. Fisher."

Not recognizing the name as his own, he was startled when the clerk leaned over the counter and said a little louder in his direction. "Margaret Fisher."

"Yes, that's me. Well, not me, but you know what I mean," he stammered.

Paying and picking up the bag, he took long strides back outside.

Pulling the heavy brown canvas closed, he glanced in Maggie's direction before picking up the reins. Noticing her cheeks had a pink glow troubled him. The bricks had long cooled, and the canvas lined interior did little to ward off the cold.

"You okay?"

Maggie whispered, "I'm a little chilled."

"I'm sorry I brought you out in this. I should have hired a driver."

"Don't be silly; I'm fine, and once I put my leg up, all will be well."

Not satisfied she was telling him the truth; he wasted no time arguing.

Finally, reaching South Main Street, he breathed a sigh of relief that he wouldn't need to turn again until reaching the Inn's driveway. The closeness of the buildings gave him a momentary reprieve, but as soon as they passed the sign to the Dairy Bar, the road and the farmland blended as one.

In a nervous tone, Maggie exclaimed, "Henry, I can't see the road."

"I'm counting on your aunt's horse to know the road better than me."

Trying to reassure her anxiety, he said, "How about you close your eyes and send some prayers our way?"

Without answering, she did as he asked and lowered her head.

Relieved she'd closed her eyes, he struggled to find some assurance they were still on the road. The horse slowed his trot and struggled to pull the metal-lined wooden spokes through the deepening snow. Trying to remember the distance from the Dairy Bar to the Inn, he tried to calculate how much longer it would be. Without landmarks to guide them, an empty knot formed deep in his belly. Without so much as a notice, the horse instinctively turned left, ignoring his guidance to stay straight. The sudden jerk forced Maggie's eyes open. "Oh my, where's he going?"

"I'm not sure, but I think he knows."

"Henry, where are we?"

"Somewhere between the Dairy Bar and the Inn. There are only a few houses between the Inn and town. Maybe he's been here before and knew we needed off the road."

"Let's hope so; horses are smart like that." She said.

All at once, the back end of the buggy dropped, abruptly preventing the horse from taking one step further.

Handing her the reins, he asked. "Do you think you can guide him while I push us out?"

"Yes," was all she said as she gently slid over to the middle of the bench.

Pulling his collar up around his neck, he braced himself for the snow blowing sideways in front of the buggy. Silently thanking the Lord, they didn't stop in the middle of the road; he made his way to the back of the carriage. The jagged spoke lay wedged in a hole at his feet, leaving him dismayed.

Pushing the canvas covering aside, he moved the top half of his body in the protected area and said, "I think there's a house up there. I'm going to see if anyone is home."

"I'm going with you."

"Why don't you let me check first?"

In a weak voice, she said, "I'm cold."

"Well, you're not walking."

"Henry, you can't carry me all that way, I'm too heavy."

"Doctors orders," was all he said.

Realizing she was fighting a battle she couldn't win, she gave in.

The minute his cheek brushed her forehead, the hue on her face was apparent. What had he gotten them into was all he could think of as he prayed someone would be home.

Letting the faint color change guide his way, he used the robin egg blue door to act as a beacon in a sea of white. The moment he stepped foot on the porch, panic took over as he realized they had made it to the farm across from the Inn - an empty house.

Praying the door would be unlocked, he shifted her weight and turned the knob with his hand under her knees. When he met resistance, he walked to the window and looked through the house. Through the kitchen, was another door. Struggling to carry Maggie through the knee-deep snow, he was relieved the back porch was covered. Setting her down on a bench near the door, he looked around for any sign of a key.

Pointing to the milk can sitting to the right of the door, Maggie said in a quiet tone. "Maybe under there?"

"Thank the Lord," was all he said as he found a key and fumbled to unlock the door with his gloved hands.

Helping her stand, she took his hand as he led her inside. The sparsely furnished kitchen held no life, but it's wood floors, and oak cupboards warmed the cold room. Pulling a chair out for her at the long farmhouse table, he looked for a way to bring light to the room. Retrieving a long match from the holder secured to the wall near the stove, he removed the glass flu from the lantern and turned the wick up enough to ignite a glow over the table.

Maggie's body shook as he removed his coat and wrapped her in another layer before heading back to the porch. In the far corner sat a stack of wood, and he loaded his arms and grabbed the small hatchet leaning up against the wall. Dropping the logs in front of the white porcelain cookstove, he chipped tiny slivers of wood and positioned them in the firebox before lighting them.

The barren house did little to ease his anxiousness in making Maggie comfortable. Once the fire was warming the cast iron stove top, he headed to the stairs. Taking them two at a time, he prayed there would be something left behind. The long hallway at the top of the stairs presented several doors meant for a growing family. Opening the first one, he was relieved to find an empty bed. Wasting no time in carrying the child's size mattress to the kitchen, he laid it on the floor in front of the stove.

Holding his hand over the stovetop, he opened the firebox, willing it to warm the barren kitchen before saying, "Would you be more comfortable lying down?"

"I'm good sitting, but maybe I'd warm up if I sat closer to the heat," she said in a shaky voice.

Helping her stand as he moved the chair closer, he said, "I need to tend to the horse and put him in the barn. Will you be okay for a few minutes?"

Removing his coat from her shoulder, she held it out to him as she asked, "Can you bring in that bag from the drugstore?"

Holding his hand up, he said, "Keep it; you need it more than I do."

"Henry, please! I'll be fine; you have a fire started, and it'll warm up in here fast. Take care of the horse and bring me my prescription."

Without arguing, he reluctantly took his coat and headed to the door. Stepping off the porch, he walked close to the house, ducking around the trees as they bent out of shape under the snow's weight. Moving in the direction of the buggy, he unhooked the horse and moved toward the barn. Holding the horses' lead in one hand and moved the snow away from the barn door with his foot, it took a few minutes before he freed the door enough so that it would slide on its overhead track.

With filtered light spilling in through the open door, he led the horse to an empty stall and secured the latch. Rubbing his gloved hand over the horse's nose, he said, "I know, buddy, I'm hungry too. I could go for some of that French Toast Casserole Amanda was making this morning, for sure and certain. At least you'll have shelter even if I can't offer you a bucket of grain." Leaning in closer to the brown mare, he scratched his chin and patted his broad neck as he whispered, "Thanks for getting us off the road."

Chapter 17

Ginger Cookies

Henry's tracks disappeared, and the house was a faint shadow as he fought his way back to the porch. Stopping to fill the old grain bucket he found in the barn with snow, he wished he had more to offer her. Stomping off his boots and shaking the snow from his hat, a slight warmth greeted him as he opened the door.

Placing the bucket on the stovetop, he retrieved the prescription from his pocket and laid it on the table. "How are you doing?" He asked.

Opening the bag and reading the instructions on the brown bottle, she answered in a shaky voice. "My thigh is throbbing."

Pouring two pills in her hand, she said, "I've never been able to take these without water. Not sure how I'm going to swallow them."

Walking around the room and looking in each cupboard, he said, "I brought in some snow to melt and was hoping there might be a cup in here."

Turning around and leaning his hands on the counter behind him, he continued. "But it doesn't look like it." Nodding his head in the direction of the door on the opposite side of the room, he said, "I bet that's the basement, let me see if anything was left behind."

Taking a long match from the box on the wall, he opened the door and gave his eyes a moment to adjust to the darkened stairs. What light came through the snow-packed windows did little to guide his way. Locating the overhead lamp, he was grateful the oil-soaked wick burned bright. Canning shelves lined one corner of the room, and a row of empty jars sat on the bottom. Kneeling, he reached for a quart jar and was surprised to find a row of filled jars behind the empty glass containers. Pulling them out in the light, he smiled as he retrieved a jar of applesauce and peaches. Proud he'd found a treasure; he made his way back upstairs to show off his find.

Maggie moved her chair back to the table and had her head laid across folded arms. Turning her head to see what he placed in front of her, she said in a quiet voice. "Breakfast?"

In a puffed-up manner, he said as he pounded his chest. "Me man, you woman."

Hearing her soft giggle at his poor attempt at being their provider was all he needed.

Checking on the water on the stove, he asked, "You think you can wait a little longer? I want this to boil before you drink it." Opening each drawer in the kitchen, he hoped to find anything they could use.

"Payday!" He exclaimed.

He picked up each item and said with enthusiasm. "A flashlight, ink pen, playing cards, matches, tea bags, sugar packets, plastic spoons, toothpicks, ball of string, screwdriver, glue, aspirin, and a jackknife. I'd say we hit it big, don't you think?" He asked as he looked her way.

Without lifting her head, she said, "I'd say we have everything we need."

"We sure do, until I can make it over to the Inn." He said.

Picking her head up, she looked to the window and said, "You certainly aren't going to try just yet, are you? It's snowing harder than ever."

Standing at the sink and looking out over the yard, he said. "I can't even see the road. I think I'll wait until it lets up some."

"I think it's best, she replied, Looking to the filled jars on the table, she added. "Besides, the great and mighty hunter found us everything we needed."

He quite enjoyed her subdued manner, and he couldn't stop the warmth in his cheeks as she referred to him as a "*mighty hunter*." He was sure it was the fever talking, but he couldn't help but think this was a side of her he hadn't seen too much of.

Walking to her side, he laid his hand across her forehead and said, "You're a bit warm. You best take those antibiotics." Picking up the empty jar, he dipped it in the bucket and gave her enough melted snow to wash down the pills.

Taking the jar from her hand, he pulled a teabag and sugar packet from the drawer and carried them to the stove as he said, "Not too much longer, and I can make you some tea."

Pushing herself to a standing position, she whispered, "Thank you."

Rushing to her side, he asked, "What do you need?"

"I think I want to stretch my leg out. I'm going to sit down on the mattress."

Holding her elbow as she made it to the front of the stove, she lowered herself and sighed as she moved her leg to a comfortable position.

"I should've brought in the quilt from the buggy." He said as he reached for his coat and headed to the door.

"Henry, I'm fine. Quit fussing over me. You've done more than enough."

Holding his finger up and opening the door, he said, "It will only take a minute; I'll be right back."

The blinding landscape did little to guide his way to the buggy, and snow caked his pant legs to his knees. Looking in the direction of the Inn, left him no hope of walking the quarter of a mile for help. They would need to stay put until the storm passed. Brushing the snow off his pants and stomping his boots before opening the door, he said as he entered the room. "See? I was only gone a minute."

Maggie's legs were stretched out in front of her, and she had her skirt pulled up over her thigh. The fresh white gauze was stained, and a concerned looked etched in her forehead. She shivered as a gust of wind blew across her legs as he opened the door. Pulling her coat tighter and covering her leg, she said, "I think I might have ripped out a stitch or two."

Taking off his coat and laying it over the chair with the quilt, he knelt beside her and said, "Let me take a look." Rubbing his hands together for a minute before pushing her dress hem aside, he slowly peeled off the taped covering as he said, "It doesn't look like you ripped any stitches. It looks like it just bled some from being bounced around so much." Reaching for the bag on the table, he took out a fresh dressing and the antiseptic cream the doctor had recommended.

Without looking at her, he proceeded to apply new gauze and tape as tenderly as he could. He fought to keep his thoughts on the white covering and not on how her skin felt beneath his fingertips. Not in all his twenty-five years had he touched a woman so closely and twice in twenty-four hours. He was anxious to complete his task and cover her bare leg.

~~

Maggie concentrated on the top of Henry's head as he removed the tape. His rough fingers gently cared for her wound, and she couldn't care less that her thigh was uncovered in an unladylike position. The heat from her leg closely matched the warmth in her cheeks as he tenderly cared for her. She closed her eyes, dropped her chin, and tried to think of anything but the way his wet hair stuck to the back of his neck.

Pulling her hem down over her knees, he said, "There you go, good as new."

Lifting her head, she was surprised he had locked his eyes on her face and lingered for a few seconds before standing. "How about a cup of tea? The water should be plenty hot enough now. I can open the jar of the applesauce if you're hungry. Are you cold?"

Watching him bounce around the room, she let him continue to pepper her with questions as the heat in her cheeks returned to normal. If she didn't know better, she was sure their close contact rattled him as well.

Filling the empty mason jar with water, he added a tea bag and a packet of sugar before setting it on the floor beside her. Taking the quilt from the back of the chair, he held it out in front of the stove box to warm it before laying it over her legs. Walking to the drawer, he retrieved the spoons and jackknife, picked up the jar of applesauce, and sat down beside her and said, "Breakfast served."

"Perfect," was all she said as she picked up the jar of tea with two hands and brought it to her lips.

Observing him pop the metal lid with the end of the knife, he handed her a spoon and said, "My *mommi* used to make the best ginger cookies. She'd let me dip them in a bowl of applesauce. To this day, I normally can't eat one without the other."

Taking the spoon from his hand, she asked, "In applesauce?"

"I sure did. You'll have to try it. You'll never look at applesauce the same way."

Laying her spoon aside, she put her hands under the quilt and said. "It's a shame no one lives here. This kitchen is a nice size. Plenty of room for baking."

Looking around the room and toward the stairs, she asked, "How many bedrooms are upstairs?"

Leaning back on his hands and stretching his feet out in front of him, he said, "I stopped at the first door I came to. But there were three doors on one side and two on the other."

"Plenty of room," she said.

"Plenty of room for what?"

"A growing family, silly."

Nodding his head in the direction of the basement door, he added. "You should see down there. The back wall is nothing but canning shelves."

With a longing in her voice, she said, "I've always wanted a summer kitchen in a basement. It would be perfect for baking on hot days."

Curling up his eyebrows and tilting his head to the side, he said, "It wouldn't take much to add one. The whole left side is empty, with the right side taking up the washing area."

Rubbing her lower back, she asked, "Do you think you could move this closer to the wall so that I can lean back some?"

Without so much as an answer, he pulled the mattress to the wall and continued. "The barn is perfect. Stalls lined one side, and stanchion's fill the whole other side. There are pens near the back that would make a great place for a few sheep. The hayloft overhead looks good and solid, and there's even a tack room. I think there is another barn connected out back. Big enough to store a couple of buggies, I'm sure. Could be cleaned out to host church on a summer day."

She noticed the pitch in his voice change as he talked about the barn. Without giving it too much thought, she said, "You should be farming; it suits you."

As he folded his arms across his chest and crossed his feet, he said, "I have to say the more time I spend in Willow Springs, the closer I am to telling my *datt* I'm through. How about you?"

In a questioning tone, she asked, "Farming?"

Letting out a deep throat snicker before he answered, he asked, "Why aren't you baking?"

"Because like you, my *datt* has me in Willow Springs on a wild goose chase. I was perfectly happy in Tomah, but no, he thinks I need to find..." Stopping before she completed her sentence, she quickly changed the subject.

"Need to find what?" He asked.

Hesitating for a moment to find any answer but the real one she said, "A job."

"You didn't have a real job in Wisconsin?" He asked.

"I did. I was running my *mamm's* bakery and taking care of my *bruders* and *schwesters*. I was perfectly content. But my *Ddatt* though otherwise."

Letting a comfortable silence fall between them, she leaned her head against the wall and closed her eyes as he asked in a low voice.

"Do you like it here?"

Without opening her eyes, she answered, "It's growing on me, and I quite enjoy my aunts." Pausing for a moment before she continued, she asked, "And you?"

Sliding his head down on the wall until his chin met the top of her head, he said in a husky whisper. "I'm quite enjoying the company and if Bella won't come back to Indiana with me, I might stick around for a while."

The hair on the back of her neck stood up as she moved her head away from his. Turning her cheek to the wall, she fought the lump forming in the back of her throat. Trying to act as if his words hadn't burned a hole in her heart, she said in a brave voice.

"I'm going to lay down and try to take a nap."

With that, she pushed herself down and folded her arm under her head as a pillow. Pulling the quilt tight to her chin with her other hand, she closed her eyes and tried to block out the vision of him staying in Willow Springs for Bella. Right then and there, she knew there was no way she could stay. One way or another, she'd be on the first bus back to Tomah whether her family approved or not.

~~

Not sure what he said, but one thing was for certain the air in the room turned thick in an instant. Playing everything over in his head, he couldn't for the life of him figure out what he said to upset her. Moving from his place beside her, he stood and walked to the living room and stared blankly out the front window.

The empty room did little to help him understand, and he shook his head, wondering how a good conversation could turn bad in a blink of an eye. He knew he had little experience with women, but this one had him baffled.

Peering out the window, he hoped to catch a glimpse of the Inn across the street or any sign of movement on the road. A thick layer kept both hidden from view. With nothing to do but wander from window to window, he headed upstairs, hoping to let Maggie sleep.

It was apparent every inch of the home had been well cared for as he walked in and out of each room. Opening the last door at the end of the hall revealed the largest of all the rooms. Walking in to look out the double windows, he could scarcely make out the shape of the barn in the distance. On a clear day, he was confident he'd be able to view all three hundred acres from the view from this one window.

Maggie's comment played in his head. *You should be farming.* Why wasn't he doing what he'd dreamed about his whole life? A part of him believed he hadn't found anyone he wanted to create a home with yet. For that reason alone, he hadn't gotten brave enough to have a heart-to-heart conversation with his family. Until he showed up in Willow Springs, it was still only a dream. Maybe if he stayed, he could talk Bella into giving up her silly notion of getting a college degree. That might be the only reason his family would let him out of his obligation to Schrock Construction.

Heading back downstairs, he quietly walked to the drawer and pulled out the pen and paper. Sitting at the table, he sketched out some ideas he had floating around in his head.

Before he knew it, late morning turned into early afternoon, and Maggie started to stir. She let out a slight moan before pushing herself to a sitting position. She pushed her *kapp* back in place and smoothed the wrinkles out of the front of her dress before looking his way.

"Did I sleep for long?" She asked in a raspy voice.

"A few hours, I suspect."

Noticing a rose-colored hue embedded on her cheeks, he thought she looked beautiful as she pulled the quilt tighter around her middle and asked. "Do we have any more tea bags? I'm freezing. Maybe a hot cup of tea would warm me up."

Alarmed at her statement as the kitchen had warmed nicely, he wasted no time in heading to the stove and pouring hot water into her jar. Working to open a tea bag, he asked, "Is it time for another antibiotic?"

"No, every eight hours."

Kneeling beside her, he handed her the hot liquid and laid the back of his palm on her forehead.

"You're burning up. No wonder you're cold. I need to cool you down. Let's get you unwrapped from this blanket for a few minutes."

In a pleading voice, she pulled the quilt closer to her neck and said, "No, please, I'm cold."

Giving in to her plea, he sat back against the wall, wrapped his arm around her shoulder and pulled her in tight to share his warmth. She snuggled her face into his shoulder and pulled the blue and yellow fabric to her chin. "Let me warm up for a minute." She whispered into his dark blue shirt.

He held her close and rubbed the back of her arm, trying to calm the little quakes her body was experiencing. Resting his chin back on the top of her head, he whispered, "We need to get your fever down, and the shivers will stop."

In a tone almost like a cry, she said, "Please just warm me up for a few minutes."

He hated to argue, but his overwhelming need to watch over her forced him to pull the blanket off her and position her back to a laying position.

"Look, let's take your coat off, and I need to find something to use to cool you down."

In a slight whisper, she said, "Scarf. Pocket."

Pulling her arms from the sleeves, he found the blue material and laid her head back down on the mattress. "I'm going for snow; I'll be right back."

"No," was all she said as she tried to hide her head back under the warmth of the quilt.

Before heading to the door, he grabbed his hat. No sooner had he turned his hat upside down to fill it, he remembered the bottle of aspirin in the kitchen drawer.

Returning to the floor, he pried the blanket away from her head and helped her to a sitting position. Opening his palm, he said, "Here, take these," and he gave her a drink before letting her lay back down. Folding the blue piece of wool in two, he packed snow between the layers and positioned it across her forehead.

She flinched from the shock against her skin but relaxed once he leaned in and spoke softly in her ear. "I promise once you've cooled down, I'll cover you back up and keep you warm."

For the next thirty minutes, he continued to cool her forehead and the back of her neck until her body temperature dropped. She didn't say a word as she drifted in and out of sleep. The afternoon turned dark, and he lost all hope of getting her back to the warmth of the Inn.

After adding wood to the stove, he sat down beside her and watched as she slept. Wisps of wheat-colored hair escaped the bun at the back of her neck and shimmered against her flushed skin. He leaned up against the wall and stretched his legs out in front of him. As he listened to her shallow breathing, his eyes got heavy. Pushing himself down, so he was lying next to her, he was startled when she snuggled in closer and whispered, "I'm still cold."

Wrapping his arm around her middle to pull her close, he rested his chin on the top of her head.

The light bouncing off the wall became dimmer as the last of the oil burnt away. Laying in the dark, he wondered if she'd remember nuzzling in so tight once her fever broke. But for the next few hours, he'd let her sleep in his arms like it was the most natural thing in the world.

Chapter 18

Chocolate Peanut Butter No-Bakes

Maggie woke without opening her eyes. Lying still, she tried to become aware of her surroundings. The warmth from being buried into Henry's shoulder gave her a moment of comfort.

When pounding on the front door forced Henry to his feet, it shook her from her dream-like state. Watching as he stumbled over a kitchen chair on his way to the front room, she sat up and used a chair to pull herself up. Warmth in her leg was still evident even in the cold room.

Sitting at the table and smoothing out the wrinkles in her dress, a hint of embarrassment filled her as Matthew Byler stood in the doorway, glaring her way.

Walking to the backdoor to retrieve his boots, Henry said. "Matthew stopped to check on your aunts this morning, and they told him about your accident. They asked him to check on you, but when we weren't at the Inn, he started to look for us."

Opening the firebox, Henry added more wood to the stove and said. "Thank the Lord, Matthew caught a glimpse of our buggy at the end of the driveway."

Hopping on one leg while trying to pull on his boot, he added. "Matthew has a shovel in the back of his buggy. I'm going to shovel a path." Holding his hand over the stove, he said, "I won't be long, and you should be plenty warm enough."

There was an uncomfortable silence in the room as she busied herself with the prescription bottle as Henry put on his coat.

From across the room, Matthew twirled his hat in his hand and, in a teasing tone, said, "Everyone is worried about you, but by the looks of it, you were snug as two bugs in a rug."

Heat rose to Maggie's cheeks, and a knot formed in her stomach at Matthew's reaction to the mattress on the floor. She was sure she would be sick. Without saying a word, she waited for Henry to set Matthew straight, but when all he did was snicker at Matthew's comment, her embarrassment turned to anger.

Wrinkles formed on her forehead as she looked Henry's way, pleading with him to stop egging Matthew on. He brushed by her, stopping long enough to look back with a smile and a wink before slapping Matthew on the back and heading out the door.

Sitting alone, she rubbed her leg as she gathered her thoughts. She couldn't imagine what her aunts would say when they found out she'd spent the night alone with Henry. The growing knot softened as she remembered how safe she felt lying next to him. But it didn't matter, as soon as her leg healed, she'd be going home. The only way of getting him off her mind was to get as far away from him as possible. Maybe then he could work things out with Bella.

~~

Treading through the snow, Henry retrieved the shovel from the back of Matthew's buggy as he said, "I'm so glad you went out looking for us. I knew we were only across the street from the Inn, but there was no way I was going to be able to carry her that far. She's been fighting a fever all night long, and I need to get her home."

Matthew pointed to the road and said, "The plows have been at it all morning, and most of the roads are clear. Once we get her home, we'll come back to fix that wheel."

Henry busied himself with making a path toward the porch as he said, "I'm sure she's going to fight me, but she's going home."

Matthew looked toward the barn and said, "It's a shame no one bought this place. I hear it's about to be bulldozed down."

Through labored breaths, Henry replied, "Not if I have anything to do about it."

"The grapevine has it that you're helping that English fellow from New York build a bakery on this property," Matthew said.

"Well, the grapevine has it all wrong; what I'm trying to do is find a way to stop him. I have a notion there's more to Mrs. Sorensen selling this land, and I'm on a quest to figure out what it might be. I've been stalling Mr. Waldorf until I can have a word or two with Mrs. Sorensen."

Matthew grabbed the shovel from Henry and started pushing snow aside as he said, "This property has more value than farmland. Years ago, a drilling company tried to buy it. If I remember right, it was about the same time Nate Beiler died in a silo accident. Not too long after that, Mrs. Sorensen grabbed it up. The community was up in arms about it. Many of us think it should have gone to an Amish family. Nobody understood why she bought it, but at the time, it helped Carlene Beiler and her eight daughters. There was no way they could take care of it all by themselves."

Taking his turn with the shovel, Henry said, "This place is growing on me."

In a questioning tone, Matthew asked, "That wouldn't have anything to do with Maggie Fisher, does it?"

In a smug voice, Henry replied, "Between her and trying to convince my *schwester* to go home, I'm inclined to stay."

"By the look she gave you in there; I'd say you have your work cut out," Matthew stated.

"I get those quite often. For some reason, one minute she's as nice as can be, and the next, she acts as if I'm the devil. I haven't been able to figure that one out yet. I suppose letting you believe there was more going on than just keeping each other warm had something to do with the daggers she threw me earlier."

Letting out a manly grunt, Matthew said. "You have to admit it looked pretty cozy in there. I'm sure the Bishop wouldn't approve in the least."

Looking up from his shovel, Henry said, "And I'll count on it; he won't be the wiser."

Running a finger across his lips, Matthew said, "Closed uptight, your secret is safe with me."

Leaning on the shovel, Henry said, "Now, don't go blowing this out of proportion. You know as good as me, nothing went on, and if I had any way of getting her out, I would've."

In a snicker, Matthew said, "In my books, it doesn't look like you tried too hard."

Passing the shovel to Matthew, he said in a convincing tone. "There was no way I could have carried her to the Inn, and you know that. Now quit assuming I had a plan and finish up. I'm going to help her to the buggy."

Throwing a shovel of snow toward his back as he walked away, Matthew said, "Whatever you need to do to sleep at night. Look, if I could spend a night holding a woman close in a storm, I would've done the same thing."

Reaching down to form a snowball, Henry threw it in Matthew's direction and said, "Quit!"

~~

Sitting at the table, Maggie unpinned her *kapp* and let loose her hair combing it with her fingers before rewinding it in a bun. The back of her head ached from keeping her hair up all night. After securing the starched white covering back to the top of her head, she pulled up her skirt to examine her wound. It still was warm to touch, but it didn't ache like it had the day before. She'd like nothing more than a clean dress, let alone a trip to the bathroom. Thank goodness the Inn was only a short distance away. Trying to push any thoughts of Henry from her mind, she worked on what she was going to tell both Mrs. Sorensen and her aunts about wanting to go home. She surely couldn't tell them she was leaving so Henry could patch things up with Bella. She'd have to come up with a good reason, but what that was, escaped her.

Hearing the stomp on the front porch long before he appeared, Maggie held her breath, hoping to calm her anxiety. Just the sight of him stirred things inside of her; she was ashamed to acknowledge.

Reaching for her coat off the back of the chair, he said, "We have a path cleared, and you should be able to make it to the buggy. Do you have everything?"

"Not much to gather, but I should wash up that pot and jar before we leave." She said as she tried to make her way to the stove.

"Don't worry about any of that. I'll put the mattress back upstairs and take care of things when I come for Lizzie's horse."

Holding her coat open, she had no choice but to let him help her. As she pulled the heavy bonnet from her pocket and tied it around her chin, he gathered up the drug store bag and the papers he had left on the table.

Limping toward the door, she firmly stated. "You're not carrying me."

Without responding to her statement, he pulled the door shut behind them and scooped her up before she had a chance to take one step off the porch.

"We'll see about that," was all he said as he made his way through the narrow path.

Stiffening her back in his arms, she said, "Why do you have to be like this? It's like you don't hear a word I say. I swear you purposely try to make me mad."

"I'd say I do a good job of it, don't ya think?"

"Ugh! I've had just about enough of you. I can't believe you let Matthew think there was more to our night than what was truly there."

Leaning in and whispering in her ear, he said, "I quite enjoyed our night together, didn't you?"

Squirming in his arms, she said, "Well, I never! If I were Bella, I'd be furious to know how you flirt. I have half a mind to tell her how you act when she's not around."

In a confused tone, he asked, "Bella? Why would she care?"

In an aspirated voice, she replied, "You love her, don't you?"

"Yes, of course." He answered in a questioning tone.

It was like someone punched her in the stomach as he declared his love for her. She resisted the urge to jump from his arms as he held her tightly, maneuvering the deep snow. Once they reached Matthew's buggy, he gently placed her high on the seat. She moved in closer to Matthew as Henry worked to pull the canvas door closed.

Matthew pulled back on the reins and asked, "Where to?"

As she started to tell him to go to the Inn, Henry interrupted and said, "Lizzie and Teena's."

Through clenched teeth, she said, "No, I need to go to work."

In a forceful tone, Henry answered. "What you need to do is go back to your aunts so they can look after that leg. You heard what the doctor said. You need to stay off it for a few days."

Not wanting to cause a scene in front of Matthew, she bit her lip as they slowly drove past the driveway of the Inn. She wouldn't admit it, but she was looking forward to the warmth of her bed. She was sure Bella had everything under control, and she'd deal with Mrs. Sorensen later.

Wringing her hands on her lap, she listened as Henry and Matthew carried on a friendly conversation as if she weren't sitting between them. Was she the only one who sensed the tension in the air? Henry's words, "*Yes, of course,*" rang loudly in her head as she remembered how his arms held her tight. A part of her felt like she had done something wrong, but why did it seem so incredibly right. How was she ever going to look Bella in the eye when she knew she was hopelessly in love with Henry? But more importantly, how could he act as if he cared for her when he claimed to love Bella? For the life of her, she would never understand how a man could toy with two women's hearts. The thought of it infuriated her, and she got mad all over again.

Pulling into her aunt's driveway, she thanked Matthew for rescuing them as she slid to the side of the seat after Henry got out. Just as she was about to step down, he once again picked her up.

"This is getting pretty old," she said in a snippy tone.

"Helping a damsel in distress is quite satisfying." He replied.

"First off, I'm not a damsel in distress, and I couldn’t care less if you find it satisfying or not. I'm not enjoying being carted around like some child."

"Well, I'd say if you don't like being treated like a child, you shouldn't do childish things, like gathering wood late at night by yourself. You could have saved us a lot of trouble had you just asked for help."

"See? So I am trouble. You said it yourself. Now put me down, I can walk."

"I'm sure you can, and I'll put you down once I get to the porch."

In a louder tone, she said, "You sure are full of yourself, Henry Schrock!"

Stopping a few steps from the front door, he released his hand from under her knees and let her feet fall to the snow. Surprised that he had released his grip from her, she stood still as he moved his head, so he was a few inches from her face and said in a stern tone.

"I'm not sure what bee got under your bonnet, but I've just about had enough of your sassy attitude. I've done nothing but be nice to you, and you insist on arguing with me every step of the way. I could have left you out in the woodshed to freeze to death, but no, I chased after you, and this is the thanks I get."

His apparent frustration froze her to the ground as she listened to him scold her. The creases on his forehead wrinkled as he locked his eyes firmly on hers.

"Don't think for a minute I'll make that mistake again. And here I thought I might stay in Willow Springs. But I'm sure this town isn't big enough for both of us."

The hair on the back of her neck stood up as she replied in a snippy tone.

"Well, you don't have to worry about us crossing paths. I'm planning on heading back to Wisconsin as soon as my leg heals enough to travel."

The color drained from his face, and his eyes softened as he said, "I suppose that's best."

He left her standing in the snow as he turned and headed back to Matthew's waiting buggy.

~~

With the sting of Henry's words still fresh on her face, she opened the door taking in how her aunt's house always smelled of chocolate and peanut butter. Forcing a smile when both Lizzie and Teena headed her way, she took off her coat and bonnet and hung them on the peg by the door.

Lizzie guided her to the oak rocker in the center of the room and said, "We've been so worried about you. Thank God you're home. We haven't thought about anything else since Henry stopped by and told us about your accident."

Pulling a quilt from the back of the other chair, Teena laid it across Maggie's lap and asked, "What did the doctor say? Did you have to get stitches?"

"I'm fine. I got a tetanus shot and some antibiotics. I go back next week to remove the stitches. Once I'm off my feet for a couple of days, I'll be good to go."

Putting her hand to her chest, Lizzie exclaimed. "Oh, thank goodness. We'll have to have Henry over for dinner to thank him for taking care of you."

Sitting up straight in her chair and smoothing the blanket over her lap, she said, "I'm sure I'm the last person he wants to have dinner with."

In a questioning tone, Teena asked, "For heaven's sake child, why would you say such a thing? He was so worried about you when he stopped for a bag. He couldn't leave fast enough to get back to you. I think you have it all wrong. I'd say Henry Schrock has a soft spot for you, and you just don't know it."

Quietly, Maggie answered, "No, you have it all wrong. He already has a soft spot for someone, and it's not me. You can get any matchmaking notions out of your head when it comes to Henry Schrock and me."

Pausing long enough to find the words she added. "As soon as I talk to Mrs. Sorensen, I'm going home."

"Your *datt* won't be happy," Lizzie said in a snippy tone.

"At this point, I don't care if he'll be mad or not. I've had enough of Willow Springs."

"But I thought you liked your job, and you were settling in quite nicely. Why would you want to give up so quickly?" Teena asked.

"There's no point in talking about it. I've already made my mind up. Now, if you will both excuse me, I'm going to go freshen up a bit."

~~

Lizzie waited until Maggie left the room before she turned to Teena and said, "Sounds like Miss Maggie is running from her heart. She reminds me of Barbara Miller. Remember when we locked her and Joseph in the supply room at Shetler's Grocery?"

Teena smiled and said, "I sure do, and it only took forcing them to talk for them to work things out. It looks like we might have to find out who Maggie thinks he's interested in other than her. The way I see it, only a boy who has a plan would go out of his way to take such good care of a girl."

Lizzie headed back to the kitchen as she said over her shoulder. "Come, lets' put our heads together and figure out a plan to hurry things along before she goes off and does something crazy like buying a bus ticket home."

Chapter 19

Shoofly Cake

Mrs. Sorensen sat at her desk, tapping her pencil on the pad in front of her while she waited for Mr. Waldorf to take a breath. In a louder than needed voice, he said, "Look, you agreed to sell me that land, and I don't understand why you're having second thoughts. I've already had plans drawn up for the Bakery, and if Schrock Construction doesn't build it for me, I have plenty of other English contractors that will."

In a calm but stern tone, she replied, "George, you and I have been friends for years, and I did agree to sell to you only because I thought the bakery was an excellent way to drive traffic to the Inn. I even thought it might be good for my Amish neighbors to bring in some tourists to support their cottage businesses."

"Exactly what I'm talking about," he said as he relaxed in his chair. "I predict it would be good for Lawrence County. The tourist money the Bakery and Amish Home Goods Store would bring in could have a significant impact on the community."

Sitting back in her chair, she laced her fingers and rested her elbows on the arms and said, "I went to Pittsburgh to consult with my attorney." Pausing for a moment to gauge his reaction, she continued. "He discovered a few facts that helped me understand your interest in this property."

Pushing the manila folder across the desk, he replied in a rushed tone. "My only interest in this property is helping you put feet in beds. You know as well as I do my project will bring people off the Interstate and right to your front door. All you need to do is sign the contract."

Opening the folder, she hesitated when she saw the yellow arrow indicating where her signature was needed. The line clearly stated she was signing all land and mineral rights to Waldorf Bakery Co. In an instant, her late husband's voice rang in her head. *"That piece of property is a gold mine. If it ever comes up for sale, we're buying it."* At the time, he said it in passing, and she'd never given it much thought. However, after he died and her friend Carlene's husband passed, she grabbed it up, hoping to use it as an investment. It was only after talking to her lawyer she realized what her husband was referring to about it being a gold mine. Now with the Inn experiencing a downturn in reservations, she was forced to sell.

Closing the folder, she sat back in her chair and asked, "What's your connection with Hallman Energy?"

Watching as he shifted in his chair, he took a deep breath and exhaled before saying. "I own stock in Hallman, but my involvement with them is none of your concern."

"It is if you're planning on drilling for gas. I do business in this community, and if my neighbors find out I sold to a mining company instead of an Amish family that could farm the land, it's not going to go over well. I only agreed to sell you this property in hopes it would help my business, but I'm uneasy about your true intentions."

In a gruff voice, Mr. Waldorf said, "It's none of your business what I do or don't do with this property, but I plan to build something that will bring people to the Apple Blossom Inn. Isn't that what you want in the end, to increase your reservations? You're never going to do that hidden off the beaten path and far away from the Interstate. My investors have deep pockets and can launch an advertising campaign that would encourage people to venture into Willow Springs. As far as I see it, you haven't been able to do that on your own. Let my people help you create a buzz about this sleepy little town, and I'm sure it will pad your pockets. Otherwise, all your future holds is closing your doors for good."

She opened back up the folder and picked up her pen just as the intercom on her desk buzzed in. "Mrs. Sorensen, I'm sorry to bother you, but there's a reporter in the sitting room with a camera crew who wants to speak to you."

In an aggravated tone, she gave Bella instructions. “Ask Amanda to fix a tray of sticky buns and something to drink. I'll be right out."

Closing the folder and pushing it in his direction, she said, "I need to think about this more. Let me see what these reporters want. We can finish this discussion later."

Sliding the folder back in front of her, he said in a stern tone. "I'm running out of time and patience with you and this whole project. You have to understand you can't compete with the hotels around the Outlet Mall on your own. The only way to save your precious Inn is to sell that land to me." Pausing for a moment before he continued, he said in a condescending tone. "Look, I know your husband left you deep in debt."

In a shocked voice, she asked, "How do you know that?"

Sitting back in his chair, he answered smugly. "You're not the only one who has an investigating lawyer in their back pocket. I also know it took all you had to finance the purchase of those three-hundred acres. You put the Inn up as collateral, and it's just about bankrupt you. You're at the end of your ropes, and you don't have any other options than to sell to the highest bidder, and that's me. Try to get that kind of money from any two-bit Amish farmer."

Opening the folder and pulling out the contract, she tore it in half and said, "I've had about enough of your sneaky conniving ways. I wouldn't sell you that piece of property now if my life depended on it. I'll take my chances with a two-bit Amish farmer before I sell it to you and your sneaky investors.”

Standing and slapping his hands on the desk, he boldly said, "I've had it! You and this town are going to be sorry you didn't take me up on this offer. Once the town leaders find out you've shut the door on this project, it will be on your shoulders, not mine. You can kiss your precious Inn goodbye. I'll see to it."

Mrs. Sorensen sat back in her chair as he stormed from her office. The pictures on the wall rattled as he closed the door behind him. Swirling her chair around to face the window, she took a deep breath, thinking she'd lost any hope of saving the Inn from imminent doom.

Watching the birds peck at the seeds under the feeder, she glanced around the courtyard, taking note of how the sun had melted the last of the snow from the storm a few days earlier. It was the sun shining through the trees that reminded her how her husband had always said things looked the bleakest amid a storm, but new dawn meant fresh starts. For the last few months, she'd been uptight and curt with everyone around her. But at that very moment, a renewed sense of optimism filled her. The uneasiness she'd experienced with George was replaced with a determination to find a way to save the Inn.

~~

It had been three days since Henry and Matthew dropped Maggie off, and she spent a good part of those days in her room. She was adamant she was going home, and no amount of pleading from them would change her mind. Pulling the quilt over her head, she blocked the early morning rays that were enticing her up.

A soft knock on the door announced Lizzie and Teena as they walked to the foot of her bed. "Okay, enough is enough," Lizzie said as she pulled the quilt from the bed. "We've let you mope around here for days; it's time to face your future whatever that might be."

Pulling herself to a sitting position, she said in a raspy voice. "I've not been moping."

"What do you call it then?" Teena asked.

"I've been thinking," Maggie answered as she stood and grabbed her dress off the peg by the dresser.

"Thinking or not, it's time to get back to the real world," Teena said as she handed her an envelope. "This was delivered this morning."

Taking the pink embossed envelope from her hands, she wrinkled her forehead and asked, "Who brought this?"

"Amanda dropped it off on her way to work. We let you sleep another hour or so, but it's time you get out of this funk and get back to life."

Sliding her finger along the seal to open it, she walked to the window and held the handwritten note to the light.

Margaret,

I request your return to work. There is much we need to discuss. I expect you in my office promptly at 10:00 am.

Mrs. Sorensen

Laying the note on the dresser, she said. "Ready or not, I've been summoned to Mrs. Sorensen's office. I best find a way to tell her I'm not coming back to work."

In a distressed tone, Lizzie said. "There's no reason for you to go home. I don't understand what's gotten into you. I thought you enjoyed working at the Inn, and you've made friends here. Amanda and Bella, and what about Henry?"

Pushing them both to the door, she said in a snippy tone. "Ugh, would you both stop with Henry and let me dress."

Closing the door and leaning back on it, she laid her head on the polished wood. Behind darkened eyes, Henry's face was as clear as if he were standing in front of her. There was no doubt she'd fallen for his boyish charm, and no matter how hard she tried to push the image away, his face wouldn't leave her thoughts. *If this is what love feels like, I'd sooner come down with the flu. How am I ever going to face Bella?* She thought.

Pushing herself away from the door, she whispered under her breath. "It's time I get this over with."

~~

Lizzie whispered over Teena's shoulder as they both made their way down the hallway and back into the cozy kitchen. "Looks like our visit to Mrs. Sorensen paid off."

Leaning in closer, Teena said, "Thank goodness; she agreed to help. Now, all we need to do is find a way to convince Henry."

Picking up a cup from the table, Lizzie carried it to the stove to warm up her tea and said, "What's got me stumped is why Maggie isn't following her heart. I don't understand what she's thinking."

Shaking her head as she stirred honey into her cup, Teena replied in a confused tone. "Makes no sense to me. But if Mrs. Sorensen can keep her at the Inn, it'll give us more time to work on Henry."

"Work on Henry? What are the two of you up to?" Maggie said as she stood in the doorway, hands planted boldly on her hips.

Looking toward her *schwester* and then back to Maggie, Teena added. "Work on Henry to help us fix the porch."

Lizzie handed Maggie a cup of hot water, as she said, "That's right; we need to tear off the porch and build a new one. The boards are rotten and need to be replaced. We figured there was no one better to help us than Henry."

"I'm sure there are other men in the community that are better suited for such a job. Henry's family owns a big construction company, and I'm sure a little home repair job isn't in the scope of what they do." Maggie said in a disgusted tone.

"I wouldn't be so sure of that," Lizzie added.

Sitting at the table and seeping a teabag in her cup, Maggie replied. "It doesn't matter. I'm going home soon, so if you can talk him into fixing the porch, so be it. I won't need to be around his two-timing charm."

"Two-timing charm?" Teena asked in a confused tone. "What on earth are you talking about?"

Pushing her cup away, Maggie stood and walked to the door. "Never mind, it doesn't matter. All I know is as soon as I get away from Willow Springs, the better."

Lizzie followed her to the front room as she asked in a more than forceful manner. "What is it you have against Henry? He seems like a nice young man. I've seen some hard-headed women in my days, but you beat all. You're never going to find a husband if you carry that chip around on your shoulder."

Taken back by Lizzie's tone, Maggie stopped in her tracks and said, "Henry Schrock is not who you think he is. He's a womanizer, a flirt, and not husband material. Now, if you both don't mind, I don't need your help in finding a husband, and I'll be telling Bella what kind of man he is. That's for sure."

The door clattered as it closed, leaving Lizzie turning to her sister to ask. "Why is she so concerned with telling Bella what kind of man he is?" Shaking her head, she continued, "I don't know about that girl."

Teena busied herself with gathering the ingredients for the Shoofly Cake she was baking and said, "I don't know either, but I'm not giving up just yet. If Mrs. Sorensen can convince her she needs her help, we might have some more time to work on both of them."

~~

Maggie squared her shoulders and lightly knocked on Mrs. Sorensen's open door. Waving her in and pointing to the chair across from the desk, Maggie followed the woman's instruction and patiently waited until she finished her phone call. Her chest tightened as she toyed with the exact words she'd use to tell her she was leaving.

Without missing a beat in her conversation, Mrs. Sorensen pushed a clipboard across the desk for Maggie to read. Glancing at the list, she was surprised all her duties had changed. Ordering supplies and checking in guests had changed to planning next week's menu and organizing the kitchen pantry. Tipping her head in Mrs. Sorensen's direction, the woman held up a finger to tell her she'd explain in a minute.

Picking up the list to examine it more closely, a sudden surge of excitement replaced the uneasiness of leaving her job. As far as she could tell, Mrs. Sorensen had put her in charge of everything in the kitchen. What about Amanda? She surely hoped she hadn't let her go.

Before she'd even put the phone back in its charging station, Mrs. Sorensen replied in a sharp tone. "We have much to do. I have changed things up around here in your absence. Amanda is in charge of housekeeping, Bella is in charge of marketing and guest services, and I've moved you to the kitchen. Do you have any problem with that?"

Not sure how much she could question her; Maggie took a few seconds before responding. "No, but can I ask why?"

Mrs. Sorensen sat back in her chair and said, "For one, the sticky buns you made last week were a hit with that group of women from Pittsburgh. They enjoyed their stay so much they sent a camera crew here to film the Inn. They were coming home from a Tourism Conference when the storm stranded them. You all took such good care of them; they wanted to do a story on us."

Stopping for a second to write something on the pad in front of her, she continued. "Bella told me how she used the Internet to advertise our rooms. I had all of you girls in the wrong positions." Looking over the rim of her glasses, she said in a dismissing tone. "Anything else?"

Maggie stumbled on her words as she said, "I need to talk to you about something." Without looking up, Mrs. Sorensen replied. "Not now, I have too much to do, and so do you."

When Maggie didn't move from her chair, Mrs. Sorensen sat up straight and said, "Look, I'm going to be frank with you. I need each of you girls to pull your weight around here; if not, there will be no Inn and no job to come to. I'm counting on this article in the Pittsburgh Travel Magazine to revitalize the Inn. Bella convinced me to let her use the things she learned in her marketing class to advertise the Inn. One of those things is highlighting your baking."

In a questioning tone, Maggie asked, "What about Mr. Waldorf's Bakery, how will we ever compete with that?"

Mrs. Sorensen cleared her throat before responding. "I figured out Mr. Waldorf's intentions were not in the best interest of the Inn, and he'll be taking his project elsewhere. My only intention was to save the Inn, and without his project, it will be up to us to find ways to keep the doors open."

There was something about the way Mrs. Sorensen's voice softened when she spoke about saving the Inn that touched Maggie's heart. No matter how badly she wanted to go home, she couldn't let her or the Inn down just yet.

Without saying another word, she picked up the clipboard and left the office. Studying the list, she glanced up when movement at the end of the hallway caught her attention. Stopping in her tracks, she watched as Henry wrapped his arms around Bella and rested his chin on the top of her head. The brown leather suitcase at his feet told her all she needed to know. In a hushed tone, Bella said. "I'm sorry I've disappointed you, and someday I hope you'll find it in your heart to forgive me."

Henry pushed her back and lifted her chin with a finger and said. "I understand, and in time they will too." With that, he laid a soft kiss on her forehead and reached for his bag.

Embarrassed she'd been caught watching them; Maggie's feet stayed frozen to the floor. In a quick second, Henry looked her way, held her gaze for a moment before he turned to walk out the door. No wink, no goodbye, not even a smile left her heartbroken.

Both she and Bella stood looking at the door as the man they loved walk out of their lives.

Maggie's plan to tell Bella what kind of man he really was, faded as the notion to save the girl from the truth surrounded her.

Chapter 20

Apple Roll-Ups

For the next few weeks, Maggie immersed herself in trying new recipes and organizing the kitchen to her liking. Mrs. Sorensen had given her full reign to do whatever she wanted, and she loved her new assignment. Bella had fallen into being Mrs. Sorensen's assistant, a job that better suited her, and Amanda hummed her way through her duties. Even Mrs. Sorensen's brassy exterior had softened with the onset of more reservations. She spent less time in her office and more time tasting Maggie's baked goods and watching over Bella's shoulder. The article in the Pittsburgh magazine had drawn attention to both the quaint little Inn and Maggie's sticky buns and apple roll-ups.

During the day, time went by fast, but at night when Maggie was alone with her thoughts, a sadness came over her. Every time she closed her eyes, Henry's face invaded the darkness, and a yearning for his arms around her left an ache inside, not even sleep could dull. It wasn't until the day Mrs. Sorensen stopped her as she passed her office that the depth of how she treated him came to light.

"Margaret, can you give these to the girls before you leave? I need to place this order before The Mercantile closes." Maggie took the envelopes and headed back to the kitchen. She knew Bella and Amanda were sitting at the table, enjoying a cup of tea before they left for the day. She'd been so busy she'd forgotten it was payday.

Looking down and reading the names, she moved hers to the bottom of the stack, handed Amanda hers, and stopped when she read the last one out loud in a questioning tone. "Bella Schrock."

"Yep, that's me," Bella said as she took the envelope from Maggie's hand. In a hushed tone, Bella said, "Really, my name is Annabella, but don't tell Mrs. Sorensen, or she'll insist on calling me that."

Like placing the last few pieces of a puzzle together, Maggie asked, "Why did I think your last name was Fleming?"

Bella placed her hand over her mouth and snickered before saying. "Probably because I introduced myself as Bella Fleming. I know it's silly, but when I first moved here, I didn't want people to know I was Amish. I wanted to fit in with my English friends, so I pretended my name was Fleming." Pausing to take a sip of tea before continuing, she said in a longing tone. "Fleming is such a pretty name, don't you think?"

Amanda was quick to add. "All I know is you can dress English and try to pretend you're someone you're not, but the minute you open your mouth, you give it all away. What did Henry think of your little charade?"

Running her fingertip over the rim of her cup, Bella answered. "Yeah, he wasn't too happy. I had to beg him not to tell our parents. It was one thing not to come home after *Rumspringa,* but not wanting to use my given name, that might have pushed them right over the edge."

Maggie couldn't listen to one more word. Heat rose to her face as if someone had lit a match under her chin. What had she done? She'd pushed Henry away all because of a horrible mis-understanding. Turning before the girls noticed tears welling in her eyes, she said, "I gotta go."

She couldn't escape the Inn fast enough and only stopped when she'd made it to the end of the picket fence of the farm. Looking tenderly toward the house, she noticed the trees shading the porch had started to bloom. An unearthly urge to walk down the driveway and look inside one last time forced her to forge ahead.

Walking up the steps, she peered in the living room window and was surprised at several boxes sitting in the center of the room. Moving away from the window, she placed her hand on her heart to calm its racing beat. Someone had moved into the farmhouse, and a part of her couldn't help but be curious about its new occupants.

Backing away from the window, she stopped in her tracks as a voice behind her said, "Taking up being a Peeping Tom these days?" Turning to follow the sound, she gasped when she saw Henry leaning on the side of the house with arms crossed over his chest with a smug look on his face.

"Henry, what are you doing here?" She asked.

"I should be asking you the same thing."

Stuttering on her words, she said, "I... I wanted to look inside."

"All you had to do is knock, and I would've opened the door."

"What are you doing here?" She asked again.

"I suppose I have a right to be here since it's my house."

In a surprised voice, she asked, "Your house?"

"Yep, bought and paid for. All three-hundred acres."

"Why?" She asked in a shocked tone.

"Willow Springs kinda grew on me, and I promised my folks I'd keep an eye on Bella. It didn't hurt that I got a letter from Lizzie shortly after I got back to Indiana."

"Lizzie? Why would she write to you?"

"Seems like she ran into Bella at the Mercantile, and she helped her figure out a few things. The way I understand it, there's been a little misunderstanding that I needed to come back and straighten out."

“Why on earth didn’t they tell me?” A rosy pink colored her cheeks as she continued. "I thought Bella was…"

She didn't even finish her sentence before he wrapped his arms around her middle and pulled her close. Laying his finger across her lips to stop her in mid-sentence, he said, "I knew exactly what you thought, but I had things to take care of at home first."

"So, you let me believe..."

Laying his finger back on her lips, he said, "Shhh, I'm not done yet." Leaning down and softly pressing his lips to hers, he pulled back and said, "To be husband material, I needed a place to live and a way to make a living, and I only want to do those things here with you."

With pleading eyes, she looked up at him and asked, "Henry, what are you trying to say?"

"What I'm trying to say is I want you to be my wife."

Epilogue

Spring had turned into early October as the leaves on the apple tree shading Maggie's front porch turned a sun-kissed yellow. Cinnamon and spice filled the air as the aroma escaped the open window as she stood on the steps. Sipping her coffee, she rubbed the little mound just starting to show beneath her apron as she watched the activity across the street. The Apple Blossom Inn had become the talk of the town, as Bella helped organize an Amish Fall Festival on the grounds of the Inn. All the local cottage businesses had reserved a booth and were excited to share their handmade furniture, homegrown produce, and quilts to the public.

A group of men had set up a big copper pot over a fire and were taking turns stirring a cauldron of apple butter. A lumberjack contest was scheduled at noon, and it was all Henry could talk about at breakfast.

The screen door slammed behind her just as Henry's strong arm engulfed her shoulder.

Nodding his head in the direction of the cars lining both sides of the road, Henry said, "Looks like all of Bella's hard work is paying off. I'd say she found her place in the world, even if it means she's walked away from her faith."

Maggie leaned into his shoulder and said, "I wouldn't be so sure she's walked away forever. The right man hasn't come along yet to pull her back. She needed to explore the outside world for a little while, but I know her heart still belongs to the Amish. If you haven't noticed, she hasn't worn her hair down in months, and I haven't seen her in blue jeans in weeks."

Looking down with hopeful eyes, he said, "You're right; I didn't realize it until now. Do you think she'll come back?"

"Let's just say Ben Kaufman from the Mercantile has been hanging around longer than normal when he makes his deliveries." Wrapping her free arm around Henry's middle, she kissed his cheek and said, "Besides, it's The Apple Blossom Inn, and it won't be the first time it's helped love bloom."

Books by Tracy Fredrychowski

The Amish of Lawrence County Series

Secrets of Willow Springs - Book 1

Secrets of Willow Springs - Book 2

Secrets of Willow Springs - Book 2

The Amish Women of Lawrence County Series

Emma

Read the novella for free.
https://dl.bookfunnel.com/v9wmnj7kve

Apple Blossom Inn Series

Love Blooms

What did you think?

First of all, thank you for purchasing, "*Love Blooms at the Apple Blossom Inn.*"

I know you could have picked any number of books to read, but you chose this book, and for that, I am incredibly grateful. I hope it added value and quality to your everyday life. If so, it would be nice if you could share this book with your friends and family on Social Media.

If you enjoyed this book and found some benefit in reading it, I'd like to hear from you and hope that you could take some time to post a review on Amazon. Your feedback and support will help me improve my writing craft for future projects.

Appendix

Sugar Cookies

Ingredients:

- 1 cup powdered sugar
- 1 cup sugar
- 1 cup unsalted softened butter
- 1 cup Canola oil
- 2 teaspoons vanilla
- 2 eggs
- 5 cups all-purpose flour
- 1 teaspoon salt
- 1 teaspoon baking soda
- 1 teaspoon cream of tarter

Instructions:

- Preheat oven to 350°
- In a large bowl, cream together sugars, butter, Canola oil, and vanilla until light and fluffy. Add eggs one at a time and blend evenly. In a separate bowl, sift together the flour, salt, baking soda, and cream of tartar. Gradually add flour mixture to wet ingredients until combined.
- Drop rounded 2-inch balls on a greased cookie sheet. Flatten balls with the bottom of a glass dipped in sugar. Bake for 10 to 12 minutes, until edges, turn a golden brown. Allow cookies to cool on cookie sheet for 2 minutes before transferring to a wire rack.
- Makes 4 dozen cookies

Honey White Wheat Bread

Ingredients:

- 2 1/2 teaspoons dry yeast
- 1/2 cup warm water (110° to 115°)
- 2 cups milk at room temperature
- 1/3 cup honey
- 2 teaspoons salt
- 2 1/2 tablespoons oil
- 2 cups wheat flour
- 4 1/2 - 5 cups bread flour

Instructions:

- In a large bowl, dissolve yeast in warm water. In a separate bowl, add two cups of wheat flour, salt, honey, and oil. Add yeast mixture and beat until smooth. Stir in enough remaining bread flour, alternating with milk to form a soft dough.
- Turn onto a floured surface; knead until smooth and elastic, about 8-10 minutes. Place in an oiled bowl, turning once to oil the top. Cover and let rise in a warm place until doubled.
- Punch dough down. Turn onto a lightly floured surface; roll out with a rolling pin and roll out any air bubbles, divide dough in half. Shape each into a loaf. Place in two greased 9"x5" loaf pans. Cover and let rise until doubled.
- Bake at 350° for 30-35 minutes or until golden brown and bread sounds hollow when tapped. Remove from pans to wire racks to cool.

Vanilla Scones

Ingredients:

- 2 cups all-purpose flour
- 2 tablespoons sugar
- 1 tablespoon baking powder
- 1/2 teaspoon kosher salt
- 6 tablespoons unsalted cold butter
- 1 small box instant vanilla pudding mix
- 1 tablespoon pure vanilla extract
- 1 large egg
- 1 cup plus 1 tablespoon heavy cream, divided

Glaze

- 1 cup powdered sugar
- 1 tablespoon pure vanilla extract
- 2-3 tablespoons heavy cream

Instructions:

- Preheat oven to 425°. Line a baking sheet with parchment paper.
- In a large bowl, whisk together the flour, sugar, baking powder, and salt.
- Using a pastry blender, cut in cold butter until it resembles crumbs.
- Mix in the pudding. With a spoon, make a well in the center of the mix and add vanilla, egg, and ½ cup cream.
- Gently stir until just combined and forms a ball.
- Turn dough onto a lightly floured surface and form into two small disks and ½ inch thick. Cut each round into eight triangles and place each on the prepared baking sheet.
- Brush each triangle with the remaining one tablespoon heavy cream.

- Bake for 8-10 minutes until just golden. Cool completely before frosting
- To make the glaze; mix powdered sugar, vanilla, and two tablespoons cream. Add more cream as needed for desired consistency. Lightly drizzle glaze over scones.

Apple Crisp

Ingredients:

- 6 large Granny Smith apples
- 1 cup quick oats
- ¾ cup brown sugar
- ½ cup flour
- ½ cup cold butter
- 2 teaspoons cinnamon

Instructions:

- Preheat oven to 350°
- Peel and thinly slice apples and place in 9"x9" square baking dish.
- Add remaining ingredients in a mixing bowl.
- Using a pastry blender, cut cold butter into mixture until it resembles coarse crumbs.
- Bake for 30 minutes.

Blueberry Muffins

Ingredients:

- 2 cups all-purpose flour plus 1 tablespoon
- 3 teaspoons baking powder
- 1/2 teaspoon salt
- 2 large eggs
- 1 cup granulated sugar
- 1 teaspoon pure vanilla
- 1/2 cup vegetable oil
- 1 cup sour cream
- 2 1/4 cups fresh or frozen blueberries

Crumb Topping:

- 3/4 cup all-purpose flour
- 2/3 cup brown sugar
- 4 tablespoons butter melted
- 1-2 teaspoons cinnamon

Instructions:

- Preheat oven to 400°
- Combine all crumb topping ingredients in a small bowl and set aside.
- Sift together two cups of flour, baking powder, and salt in a large bowl and set aside.
- In a separate bowl, whisk together eggs and sugar until combined. Add oil, sour cream, and vanilla and mix until combined.
- Stir wet ingredients into flour mixture until just combined. Do not over mix.
- In a small bowl, add blueberries and toss with one tablespoon flour and gently fold into the batter.

- Fill each muffin tin about 2/3 full and top the muffins with a generous sprinkle of the crumb topping.
- Bake 18-20 minutes until muffins are lightly browned, and a toothpick comes out clean.
- Makes about 16 muffins.

Double Chocolate Brownies

Ingredients:

- ½ cup all-purpose flour
- 1/3 cup cocoa
- 1/4 teaspoon baking soda
- 1/4 teaspoon salt
- 1/3 cup unsalted butter
- 1 cup sugar
- 2 tablespoons cold-brewed coffee
- 12-ounce semi-sweet chocolate chips
- 1 teaspoon pure vanilla
- 2 eggs
- 1/2 cup chopped walnuts

Instructions:

- Preheat oven to 325°
- Combine flour, baking soda, and salt in a small bowl and set aside.
- In a small saucepan, combine butter, sugar, and coffee. Bring to a boil, then remove from heat and add 6 oz of chocolate chips and vanilla. Stir until melted.
- Transfer chocolate mixture to a large bowl and add eggs, one at a time, beating well after each addition.
- Gradually blend in flour mixture. Avoid over mixing.
- Stir in remaining chocolate chips and the nuts.
- Spread into a greased 9-inch square baking pan.
- Bake 30 to 35 minutes or until the top looks dry and the edges pull away from the side of the pan.

Chocolate Cake with Peanut Butter Frosting

Ingredients:

- 2 cups sugar
- 2 cups sifted all-purpose flour
- 1 teaspoon baking powder
- 2 teaspoons baking soda
- 1/4 teaspoon salt
- 1/2 cup cocoa
- 1/2 cup vegetable oil
- 1 cup freshly brewed hot coffee
- 2 eggs
- 1 cup whole milk
- 1 teaspoon vanilla

Instructions:

- Sift together sugar, flour, baking soda, salt, and baking powder in a separate bowl and set aside.
- In a large mixing bowl, dissolve the cocoa in the hot coffee.
- Add oil and vanilla and mix well.
- Add flour mixture to the cocoa, coffee and oil mixture.
- Stir in milk.
- Add eggs one at a time and mix well until all blended.
- The cake batter will be runny.
- Using a 9x13 cake pan, pour batter into a greased and floured pan.
- Bake at 350° for 30-35 minutes. Do not over bake.
- Let cake cool completely on a wire rack

Icing:

- 1/2 cup soft butter
- 1 cup smooth peanut butter
- 1 teaspoon vanilla

- 4 cups sifted powdered sugar

Instructions:

- With a mixer, cream together butter and peanut butter until well combined. Add vanilla and mix well.
- Slowly add powdered sugar until frosting is spreadable.

Banana Nut Muffins

Ingredients:

- 1/2 cup butter, melted
- 3.4 oz box of banana instant pudding
- 1/2 cup packed light brown sugar
- 2 large eggs
- 2 medium mashed ripe bananas (3/4 cup mashed)
- ¼ cup milk
- ¼ cup sour cream
- 2 1/4 cups all-purpose flour
- 3/4 teaspoon baking soda
- 1/2 teaspoon baking powder
- 1/2 teaspoon salt
- 1/4 teaspoon ground cinnamon
- 2/3 cup chopped walnuts or pecans

Crumb Topping

- 1/3 cup packed light brown sugar
- 2 tablespoons all-purpose flour
- 2 tablespoons melted butter

Instructions:

- Preheat oven to 350°. Generously grease or spray muffin tin.
- In a large bowl, beat pudding, butter, and sugars until fluffy.
- Add eggs, one at a time, beating well after each addition.
- Stir in mashed bananas, milk, and sour cream.
- In a separate bowl, whisk flour, baking soda, baking powder, salt, and cinnamon together.

- Alternate flour mixture and milk in egg mixture until blended until just combined. Don't over mix batter. Gently stir in chopped nuts.
- Fill each muffin cup 2/3 full.
- In a small bowl, stir together all crumb topping ingredients until combined.
- Generously sprinkle topping on each muffin batter.
- Bake 17 to 20 minutes or until wooden pick comes out clean. Let cool in the pan for five minutes before removing to cool on wire rack.

Coffee Cake

Crumb topping:

- 1 cup sugar
- 1/4 teaspoon salt
- 1 cup all-purpose flour
- 1 tablespoon cinnamon
- 6 tablespoons melted butter

Filling:

- 1 cup packed brown sugar
- 1 1/2 tablespoons cinnamon
- 1 teaspoon unsweetened cocoa powder

Cake:

- 12 tablespoons unsalted butter, at room temperature
- 1 teaspoon salt
- 1 1/2 cups granulated sugar
- 1/3 cup packed brown sugar
- 2 1/2 teaspoons baking powder
- 2 teaspoons vanilla extract
- 3 large eggs, at room temperature
- 3/4 cup sour cream at room temperature
- 1 1/4 cups milk at room temperature
- 3 3/4 cups all-purpose flour

Instructions:

- Preheat the oven to 350°. Lightly grease a 9" x 13" pan
- In a small bowl, mix all topping ingredients and set aside.
- In a separate bowl, mix all filling ingredients and set aside.
- For the cake, beat butter, salt, sugars, baking powder, and vanilla in a large bowl until smooth. Add the eggs one at a time, beating well after each addition.

- In a small bowl, whisk together the sour cream and milk until combined.
- Add the flour to the butter mixture alternately with the sour cream mixture, beating gently to combine.
- Spread half the batter into 9x13 pan.
- Sprinkle the filling over batter in 9x13 pan.
- Spread the remaining batter on top of the filling. Use a table knife to swirl the filling into the batter gently.
- Sprinkle the topping over the batter in the pan.
- Bake 55 to 60 minutes or until cake springs back when touched.

Apple Filled Moon Pies

Filling:

- 8-ounce dried apples
- ½ cup sugar
- ½ cup brown sugar
- 2 teaspoons allspice
- 1 teaspoon cinnamon

Crust:

- 3 cups all-purpose flour
- 1 ¼ cups shortening
- 1 teaspoon salt
- 1 tablespoon white vinegar
- 1 egg
- 1/3 cup cold water

Instructions:

- Soak dried apples overnight in enough water to cover apples. Place a plate on top of apples to keep them immersed in water.
- The next day, add the sugar and spices and cook the apples until soft and then mash with a potato masher until smooth.
- Cool apple mixture to room temperature.
- Make pie crust and roll out into small seven-inch circles.
- Add two tablespoons of apple filling to each circle and fold over into half-moon shape and seal.
- Bake at 350° for 35 minutes or until bottoms are brown.

Cherry Bars

Ingredients:

- 1 cup soft butter
- 1 3/4 cup sugar
- 4 eggs
- 1 teaspoon vanilla
- 1 teaspoon almond extract
- 2 1/2 cups all-purpose flour
- 1 1/2 teaspoon baking powder
- 1/2 teaspoon salt
- 1 1/2 cup cherry pie filling

Glaze:

- 1/2 cup powdered sugar
- 3 tablespoons milk

Instructions:

- Preheat oven to 350°
- In a large bowl, cream butter and sugar until fluffy. Beat in eggs, vanilla, and almond extract.
- In a separate bowl, combine all dry ingredients.
- Stir dry ingredients into creamed mixture. Reserve 1 1/2 cups of the batter.
- Pour remaining batter in a greased jelly roll pan. Cover with pie filling.
- Drop reserved batter by big spoonfuls over cherry layer.
- Bake for 40 minutes and cool for 15 minutes before drizzling glaze over bars.

Cinnamon Waffles

Ingredients:

- 2 cups all-purpose flour
- 3 tablespoons sugar
- 1 teaspoon salt
- 3 teaspoons baking powder
- 2 eggs separated
- 1 ¾ cup milk
- 4 tablespoons melted butter
- 2 teaspoons cinnamon

Instructions:

- Sift dry ingredients together. Add egg yolks and milk beat until smooth, add melted butter. Stiffly beat the 2 egg whites, gently fold egg whites into batter.
- Beat together with a mixer until smooth. This can be frozen, defrost at room temperature, when thawed, stir well.
- Preheat and prepare Waffle Iron.
- Makes about 8 waffles.
- Before serving, spread with brown sugar butter and a spoon of sweetened cream cheese to the top of the waffle.

Brown Sugar Butter - Makes about ½ cup

- Stir together 3 tablespoons of softened butter with 3 tablespoons of brown sugar until well blended. Mix equal parts of each for the needed amount.

Sweeten Cream Cheese

- 8 oz. pkg. Softened cream cheese
- 1 cup powder sugar
- 1 teaspoon vanilla

Cinnamon Rolls

Rolls:

- 2 teaspoons sugar plus 2/3 cup, divided
- 1 cup warm water
- 2 1/4 teaspoons yeast
- 4 eggs
- 2/3 cup melted butter
- 1 teaspoon salt
- 1 cup mashed potatoes
- 6 cups bread flour

Filling:

- 1 cup brown sugar
- 2 tablespoons cinnamon
- 6 tablespoons melted butter

Icing:

- 1 stick butter
- 1 cup brown sugar
- 1/4 teaspoon salt
- 1/4 cup milk
- 1 teaspoon vanilla
- 2 1/2 cups powdered sugar

Instructions:

- In a glass measuring cup, add warm water, two teaspoons of sugar, and the yeast.
- Let stand for 5 minutes until it forms bubbles.
- Add all other roll ingredients in a large bowl and add the yeast mixture slowly.
- Mix until well blended and knead for five minutes.
- Cover dough and let rise until doubled. (About 2 hours.)

- Punch down dough and roll out in a rectangular shape. Spread with melted butter and sprinkle cinnamon and sugar to cover.
- Roll up and cut into 1-inch slices.
- Place slices on a greased baking sheet or 8" cake pan.
- Let rise again until doubled in size.
- Bake at 350° for 20-25 minutes, or until golden brown.
- While the rolls are baking melt butter for icing and blend in the brown sugar and salt.
- Cook over low heat until sugar is dissolved.
- Add powdered sugar and vanilla and mix well.
- Allow the rolls to cool for 30 minutes before spreading a thin layer of icing on top.

Buttermilk Biscuits

Ingredients:

- 2 1/4 cups all-purpose flour
- 2 1/4 cups cake flour
- 1 1/2 teaspoons salt
- 1 1/2 tablespoons baking powder
- 1 teaspoon baking soda
- 1 cup unsalted cold butter
- 2 cups buttermilk

Instructions:

- Preheat the oven to 475°
- In a large bowl, whisk together flours, salt, baking powder, and soda.
- With a pastry blender, cut in the butter until the mixture is crumbly.
- Add the buttermilk and mix just until combined. The dough will be slightly sticky.
- Turn the dough out onto a floured board and roll out to one inch thick. Cut with a biscuit cutter.
- Place on a lightly greased baking pan with the sides just touching.
- Brush the tops of the biscuits with melted butter.
- Bake at 475° for 5 minutes, then reduce the heat to 425° and bake for an additional 8-10 minutes.

Overnight Sticky Buns

Ingredients:

Dough

- ½ cup unsalted butter
- 1 cup milk
- 5 tablespoons sugar
- 1 tablespoon active dry yeast
- 1½ teaspoon kosher salt
- 1 large egg + 1 large egg yolk
- 3 to 3½ cups all-purpose flour

Topping

- ¾ cup unsalted butter
- ¾ cup packed brown sugar
- ¼ cup light corn syrup
- ¾ cup chopped pecans

Filling

- 4 tablespoons unsalted butter
- 1 cup sugar
- 1 tablespoons cinnamon

Instructions:

- In a small saucepan, melt butter and then stir in milk and sugar. Heat until the sugar has dissolved and lukewarm. Pour into a large mixing bowl and stir in yeast. Let rest for ten minutes, then stir in salt.
- In a separate small bowl, beat whole egg and egg yolk until blended and stir into milk mixture. One cup at a time stir in flour until the dough comes together in a ball. The dough will be sticky. Pour on a floured surface and knead for five

minutes. Transfer to a greased glass bowl and cover loosely with plastic wrap. Allow to rise in a warm spot until double in size.

- Once the dough has risen, make the topping by melting the butter, brown sugar, and corn syrup in a small saucepan over medium heat.
- Grease a 9x13-inch baking pan with melted butter and pour topping mixture to cover the bottom of the pan. Sprinkle with chopped pecans and set pan aside.
- Punch down the dough and turn it on a lightly floured surface. Knead for one minute and roll into a 15x12-inch rectangle.
- Make the filling by melting four tablespoons of butter and brush over the rectangle. Mix sugar and cinnamon and sprinkle over dough. Roll the rectangle up by the long edge.
- Slice the rolled dough into 1-inch thick slices. Arrange slices cut side up over the topping mixture in the bottom of the baking pan. Cover with plastic wrap and refrigerate overnight.
- The next morning remove the pan from the refrigerator and let sit in a warm spot for one hour.
- Heat oven to 350°
- Bake until golden brown, about 35-40 minutes.
- Cool for 10 minutes before inverting pan onto a large serving tray.
- Best served warm.

French Toast Casserole

Ingredients:

- 6 slices dry bread
- 2 cups milk
- 3 eggs
- 3 teaspoons pure vanilla
- ½ cup raisins
- 3 teaspoons vanilla
- 6 tablespoons sugar
- 2 teaspoons cinnamon
- ¾ teaspoons nutmeg
- Butter for frying and dish preparation

Instructions:

- Mix two eggs, three tablespoons sugar, 1 teaspoon vanilla, and ¼ teaspoon of nutmeg in a shallow dish. Dip bread on both sides and fry on hot skittle until golden brown.
- Butter casserole dish.
- Cut bread in small pieces and toss together with remaining sugar, cinnamon, nutmeg, and raisins and put into buttered casserole dish.
- In a separate bowl, mix together milk, egg, and two teaspoons of vanilla and pour over bread pieces.
- Bake at 350°for 40 to 45 minutes until the milk is absorbed but not dry.
- Serve with a drizzle of maple syrup, warm milk or a scoop of ice cream.

Ginger Cookies

Ingredients:

- 3/4 cup shortening
- 1 cup granulated sugar
- 1 egg
- 1/4 cup molasses
- 1 cup all-purpose flour
- 1 cup wheat flour
- 1/4 teaspoon salt
- 2 teaspoons baking soda
- 1 teaspoon ground cinnamon
- 1/2 teaspoon ground cloves
- 1 tablespoon ground ginger
- Additional 1/2 cup sugar for dipping

Instructions:

- Preheat oven to 350°. Lightly grease cookie sheets.
- With a mixer, cream shortening and sugar until well blended. Add egg and molasses until combined.
- In a separate bowl, mix flour, salt, baking soda, cinnamon, cloves, and ginger together.
- Gradually add the dry ingredients to the mixing bowl on low speed until everything is incorporated and a dough forms.
- Using a small melon ball scoop, drop dough on prepared cookie sheets.
- Dip a glass bottom in sugar and lightly press each dough ball down.
- Bake for 8-10 minutes.
- Allow them to cool on a cookie sheet for a few minutes, then transfer to a cooling rack to cool completely.

Chocolate Peanut Butter No-Bakes

Ingredients:

- 2 cups sugar
- 1/2 cup milk
- 1 stick butter
- 1/2 cup unsweetened cocoa powder
- 3 cups old-fashioned rolled oats
- 1/2 cup peanut butter (smooth or crunchy)
- 1 teaspoon pure vanilla extract
- Pinch kosher salt

Instructions:

- Line a baking sheet with wax paper or parchment paper.
- Bring the sugar, milk, butter, and cocoa to a boil in a medium saucepan over medium heat, stirring occasionally, then let boil for 1 1/2 minute. Start timing as soon as it starts to boil.
- Remove from the heat. Add the oats, peanut butter, vanilla, and salt, and stir to combine.
- Drop teaspoonfuls of the mixture onto the prepared baking sheet and let sit at room temperature until cooled and hardened, about 30 minutes.

Shoofly Cake

Ingredients:

- 4 cups all-purpose flour
- 2 2/3 cup brown sugar
- 1 cup butter, cut into small pieces
- 1/8 teaspoon kosher salt
- 2 cups boiling water
- 1 cup molasses
- 2 teaspoons baking soda

Instructions:

- Heat oven to 350° and grease a 13x9 inch baking pan.
- In a large bowl, stir the flour, sugar, and salt together. Using a pastry blender add butter until it resembles crumbs.
- Measure out 1 1/2 cups of crumbs and set aside for topping.
- In a separate large bowl, combine boiling water, molasses, and baking soda.
- Add half of the liquid to the crumb mixture and mix until smooth. Add remaining liquid and mix until well blended.
- Pour the batter into your prepared pan, top with reserved crumbs. Lightly press crumbs into the batter.
- Bake 45 minutes or until a wooden pick inserted in the center comes out clean.

Apple Roll-Ups

Ingredients:

- 2 cups all-purpose flour
- 2 ½ teaspoons baking powder
- ½ teaspoon salt
- 2/3 cup cold shortening
- ½ cup milk
- 2 tablespoons of melted butter
- ½ cup brown sugar
- ½ teaspoon cinnamon
- 6 medium apples, peeled and chopped

Sauce

- 1 ½ cups brown sugar
- 1 ½ cups water
- ¼ teaspoon cinnamon
- ¼ cup butter

Instructions:

- Preheat oven to 375° and grease a 9x13 baking pan.
- In a large bowl, sift together flour, baking powder, and salt.
- Using a pastry blender to cut in shortening until it resembles crumbs.
- Add milk and work until dough forms a ball.
- Roll dough out on a lightly floured surface to ¼ inch thick.
- Spread with melted butter and sprinkle ½ cup brown sugar and ½ teaspoon of cinnamon over dough.
- Arrange chopped apples over the dough and roll up tightly on the long side.
- Cut the log into 1 ¼ inch slices and arrange cut side up in the baking pan.

- For the sauce, in a small saucepan, add brown sugar water and cinnamon and heat for five minutes, stirring constantly.
- Remove from heat and stir in ¼ cup butter until melted.
- Pour sauce over apple roll-ups in baking pan.
- Bake for 35-40 minutes.

Glossary of Pennsylvania Dutch "Deutsch" Words

Ausbund. Amish songbook.

bruder. Brother

Datt. Father or dad.

denki. "Thank You."

ja. "Yes."

kapp. Covering or prayer cap.

kinner. Children.

Mamm. Mother or mom.

Rumshpringa. "Running around" period.

schwester. Sister.

The Amish are a religious group that is typically referred to as Pennsylvania Dutch, Pennsylvania Germans, or Pennsylvania Deutsch. They are descendants of early German immigrants to Pennsylvania, and their beliefs center around living a conservative lifestyle. They arrived between the late 1600s and the early 1800s to escape religious persecutions in Europe. First settling in Pennsylvania with the promise of religious freedom by William Penn. Most Pennsylvania Dutch still speak a variation of their original German language as well as English.

About the Author

Tracy Fredrychowski lives a life similar to the stories she writes. Striving to simplify her life, she often shares her simple living tips and ideas on her website and blog at tracyfredrychowski.com.

Growing up in rural northwestern Pennsylvania, country living was instilled in her from an early age. As a young woman, she was traumatized by the murder of a young Amish woman in her rural Pennsylvania community, and she became dedicated to sharing stories of their simple existence. She inspires her readers to live God-centered lives through faith, family, and community. If you would like to enjoy more of the Amish of Lawrence County, she invites you to join her in her Private Facebook Group. There she shares her friend Jim Fisher's

Amish photography, recipes, short stories, and an inside look at her favorite Amish community nestled in northwestern Pennsylvania.

Instagram.com/tracyfredrychowski/

Facebook.com/tracyfredrychowskiauthor/

Facebook.com/groups/tracyfredrychowski/

Made in the USA
Monee, IL
05 November 2021